I stood near the edge ⎯⎯⎯⎯⎯⎯⎯⎯
sheer as I remembere ⎯⎯⎯⎯⎯⎯⎯
waves pounded agai ⎯⎯⎯⎯⎯⎯⎯

I used the rag to w ⎯⎯⎯⎯⎯⎯
When I was certain t ⎯⎯⎯⎯⎯⎯⎯
ening body under it and bent his fingers around

The fog was thicker now, a wall of gray between me and the lip of the cliff. I hoped I could see Corliss in time to jump. I made certain the car was in neutral. Then I released the emergency brake, turned on the ignition, and stepped on the accelerator.

The car darted forward. As the front wheels went over the edge the pan dropped down on the rock with a scream of tortured metal, teetering the car and springing the left rear door. The door swung forward like a flat pile driver, hitting me in the back as I jumped, slamming me down on the rock at the very lip of the cliff, my legs dangling in space, the big car beside me grinding desperately for life. On the edge of nothing.

There was a screaming in my ears. Hands clawed at me. I realized it was Corliss, tugging me back to safety as the Buick fell end over end, its headlights sweeping the sky as it plunged three hundred feet into jagged rock and white water.

I lay on the lip of the cliff, fighting for breath. Corliss lay a few feet away. In her struggle to keep me from going over the cliff, the low neckline of her dress had slipped down over one shoulder, half exposing her breast. As I watched, Corliss pulled the dress still farther down on her shoulder, and her upper lip curled away from her teeth. She hooked the fingers of my hand in her bodice.

"Take it off, Swede," she pleaded...

HOME *is* the SAILOR

by **Day Keene**

A HARD CASE CRIME NOVEL

A HARD CASE CRIME BOOK

(HCC-007)

March 2005

Published by

Dorchester Publishing Co., Inc.
200 Madison Avenue
New York, NY 10016

in collaboration with Winterfall LLC

This book is a work of fiction. Names, characters, places, and incidents either are the products of the author's imagination or are used fictitiously, and any resemblance to actual events or persons, living or dead, is entirely coincidental.

ISBN 0-8439-5356-X

Printed in the United States of America

Visit us on the web at www.HardCaseCrime.com

HOME IS THE SAILOR

Chapter One

It was night. It was hot. The sea wasn't far away. But I wasn't on it, I was near it. I could hear rollers breaking on a beach. And between me and the sea the swish of fast moving traffic.

I was lying in blood or sweat. Liquid trickled down the cords of my neck and got snared in the hair on my chest. The air was as humid as it was hot and filled with the cloying fragrance of night-flowering nicotiana. It smelled like a funeral parlor.

I sat on the edge of the bed and fought a spell of dry heaves. I wished I had a drink. I wished I knew where I was. I knew that I was naked. The chances were that I was broke. A farm. That was a laugh. I'd be standing watch on the bridge of some wallowing freighter until they sewed me in canvas.

I felt through the dark for a lamp and found one. There was a table beside the bed. It was a small table. Just big enough for a bottle of rum, a glass, an ash tray, and some cigarettes. I drank from the neck of the bottle. Then I lit a cigarette and lay back, still drunk, wondering how big a fool a man could be.

I was in a tourist-court cottage of some kind. Outside the window, on the drive, a woman wanted to know if the cottages had inner-spring mattresses.

A girl's voice said they had.

I wove to the window and looked out through the Venetian blind. I was in a first-class motel. The cottages were stone and fancy brick built in a U around a landscaped court. On the far side of the court I could see a lighted bar with a huge purple neon parrot perched on the slate roof. A half-dozen spotlighted palms fronted on U.S. 101. Across the highway was the sea. Up two cottages on the drive a pretty brunette in her early twenties was talking to a hatchet-faced dame standing beside a car with Iowa license plates. As I watched them the hatchet-faced one asked the brunette if the cottages were clean and how much it would be for one night for two adults and two children.

I didn't like her looks. I didn't like her voice. It rasped. I walked back to the bed and drank from the bottle again.

I hadn't the least recollection of checking into the court. I forced myself to think.

The last of the cargo had gone over the side at ten o'clock. What day? I'd kissed Ginty, the company agent, and the line good-by a few minutes before noon. That had been in the company's dock office in San Pedro. I was through with the sea. This time I meant it. I'd saved my pay for three years. I was going home. I was going to buy a farm, get married, and settle down.

Ginty had been in his cubbyhole, raising hell with someone over the phone. When I'd told Grace, his secretary, she'd stopped beating her typewriter. Shocked.

"You're sick, Swede," she'd accused.

"Of an old sickness, baby," I'd told her. She'd wanted to know if I had picked the girl. I'd told her not yet.

Then Ginty had come out of his cubbyhole, swearing.

8

"God Almighty. First that nitwit on the City of Boston gets stuck for eighteen thousand dollars' demurrage. Now you happen to me. What do you mean, you're quitting the sea?"

"Just what it sounds like," I'd told him.

And gone away from there. Carrying my sea bag on my shoulder. My heels thudding on planking, then cement. Smelling new coiled hawsers, white-hot metal, tar. Hearing the snick of chipping hammers, the suck of the tide around the pilings, the watch on the S.S. Lautenbach striking eight bells. Twelve o'clock noon in San Pedro. Five P.M. in Amsterdam. One A.M. tomorrow in Hong Kong. Wondering if I *could* quit the sea, after eighteen years.

I'd checked into a small hotel. I'd bought a bus ticket for Hibbing, intending to leave San Pedro at midnight. I'd had a few drinks in a bar. I'd seen a movie and had dinner. I remembered a brunette and a redhead. Both of them on the prowl. Both of them run-of-the-Simmons. Typical overweight water-front dames with thick thighs and flabby running lights. I'd bought them a few drinks for kicks. Then what?

More of it was coming back now.

I'd moved on down the highway to a joint near Laguna Beach. Drinking heavier now. My money in my belt. Spending what I had in my pocket.

I remembered sounding off about some headline in the evening paper. Something about the body of some rich guy in Chicago being found when all of his friends had thought he'd been in Europe for three years. Back of the Iron Curtain. And now the F.B.I. was looking for his

9

wife. Both the barman, a lad named Jerry, and myself had agreed we wouldn't want the F.B.I. on our tails.

Then, sometime, there'd been a crap game. In the back room of the bar. With two avocado ranchers, some construction stiffs just back from Guam, and a greasy-haired Mexican pimp. I hadn't been able to lose for winning. I'd had money in all my pockets. Three or four thousand dollars. On top of the twelve thousand in my belt.

Now I didn't even have any pockets. The thought made me sad. I'd never been so sad. I watered my sadness with rum, listening to the dame with the nasal voice arguing about the rate. She thought eight dollars for five people was too high. I wondered what she wanted for her money, oysters in her beer and dancing boys?

Then there had been a fight. I remembered the fight distinctly. The Mexican had accused me of switching dice. He'd pulled a sap, shouting, "Kill the big Swede!"

And he and the construction stiffs had tried. But a lot of lads with cracked skulls had tried that. Men who were good at the business. In Mozambique. In Alexandria. In Tangiers. With brass knuckles and curved knives.

Then what had happened? I tried to remember, and couldn't.

Outside on the drive the penny-pinching dame decided not to take the cottage. She said she thought she could get one cheaper closer to L.A.

There was a grind of gears. Wheels crunched on gravel. In the hot silence that followed the departure of the car, the smell of the nicotiana seemed even sweeter. I could hear the whir of a sprinkler. The *re-teat, re-teat* of cicadas was added to the swish of fast-moving traffic and the slap of the waves on the beach. Then high heels tapped across the wooden porch. The spring on the screen door screeched like an angry cat. The brunette I'd seen on the drive came into the cottage, smoking a cigarette. My lack of clothes didn't seem to shock her.

"How you feeling, sailor?" she asked.

"Fine," I lied. "Just fine."

I hadn't paid much attention to her. Not half enough. Her hair was brown and straight. Her cheeks were flat, her cheekbones high. She was striking rather than pretty. Her yellow two-piece bare-midriff play suit accentuated her figure. It was as nice as her smile. The top half of her breasts were bare and straining against her bodice. Her stomach was concave. She curved in in back, then out. The skin I could see was tanned, as if she spent a lot of time in the sun.

I patted the bed. "Come here."

Her smile turned wry. "Any port in a storm, eh, sailor?" She lifted her hair away from the back of her neck. "What would Corliss say?"

"Who's Corliss?" I asked her.

She came part way into the room. "You don't even remember her, huh?"

"No," I admitted. "I don't. What's the name of this joint?"

"The Purple Parrot."

The name meant nothing to me.

Her smile turned nice again. "Just get paid off, mate?"

I lighted a cigarette from the butt of the one I was smoking. "That's right."

"What ship?"

11

"The S. S. Lautenbach."

"Long trip?"

"Three years."

"No ports?"

"Only in the islands. We got caught on a shuttle run when that business in Korea started."

"Oh," she said. "I see."

"What's your name?" I asked her.

She said, "Mamie."

"I'm Swede Nelson," I told her.

I wanted to ask her who Corliss was, what kind of joint I was in, if she knew whether I had any money. And if I hadn't, what had happened to it. But something about her stopped me.

She wet her lips with the tip of her tongue and gave me a long once-over. From my feet to my bandaged head. Pausing where her fancy pleased her. Not the way most women look at a man. The way most men look at a woman. Appraising. Weighing. Speculating. I patted the bed again.

She was breathing harder than she had been. "I'm tempted, Nelson," she said. "Believe me. I've watched you sleep all day."

"Then why not?"

She said, "For various reasons."

Her eyes were gray and smoky, like ashes over a wood fire. They made me feel like a fool.

I said, "Do one of two things, will you?"

She asked, "What?"

"Either come here or get out."

Her smile turned wry again. "I think I'd better go. But

if I were you, mate, I'd get dressed and walk over to the bar."

I asked her why I should.

She said, "For some food to cushion that rum. You were drunk when Corliss brought you here. You're not much soberer now." The taut spring screeched as she opened the screen. Then she closed the screen door and came back. All the way to the bed this time. "No," she said. "Don't do it. You look like a nice guy, Swede. The kind of guy I used to think maybe I'd meet someday. Where were you headed when you got drunk?"

I told her, "Hibbing, Minnesota."

"Why?"

"To buy a farm. To get married."

Her eyes searched mine. "Then get out of here, Swede. Don't even stop at the bar."

"Why not?"

"Because I'm telling you."

I got to my feet and pulled her to me. "Look, honey—"

Breathing as hard as I was, she said, "No. Please. Don't. The screen's unlocked."

I said, "To hell with the screen," and kissed her.

She crushed her lips against mine, then pushed me away and slapped me. "Men," she said. "Men." Like it was a dirty word.

Then the spring screeched again. She was gone.

I drank from the bottle again. Then I looked in the clothes closet of the cabin. My uniform was hanging on a hanger. Someone had washed and ironed my shirt. My shoes were shined.

I looked in the pockets of my coat. Then in and under

13

the bed. My papers were intact, but my money belt was gone. So was the money I'd made in the crap game.

I even looked in the bathroom. There was a safety razor and some brushless shaving cream. I shaved and showered, staying under the cold water a long time. Then I put on my shorts and skivy and walked back and sat on the bed.

The name Corliss was vaguely familiar. I tried to tie a girl to the name.

The Mexican had accused me of cheating. He had yelled, "Kill the big Swede!" He and the construction stiffs had tried. Then what had happened?

Then I remembered Corliss. Gold and white and smiling. I began to breathe hard even thinking of her. God almighty. Of course. How could I forget Corliss? How could any man, drunk or sober, forget her?

The whole of the night just past came back.

Chapter Two

She'd come in right after the fight. Or maybe while it was still going on. But the first time I had seen her was when she had sat down in the booth.

Blonde. And tiny. And pretty. Wearing a white off-the-shoulder evening gown. With a white rose in her hair. She'd laid her hand on mine. Smiling. Her voice was as nice as the rest of her.

"What's the matter, mate? They pushing you around?"

She'd laughed with me, not at me. I'd liked her from the start. I'd offered to buy her a drink. She said that she'd like that, but wasn't I pretty drunk already?

To prove how sober I was, I drank another double rum. Then there was a gap. I tried to remember leaving the bar with her. I couldn't. The next thing I remembered was riding in an open car, the wind whipping my face. The little blonde was doing the driving. I asked her where we were going.

She glanced sideways at me, smiling. "Home," she said.

And that was fine with me.

I remembered the fragrance of flowers and the shrill of cicadas as she parked the car. My bus had been gone for hours. Dawn wasn't far away. I lurched into a cabin after her, intent on only one thing. Corliss. Sure. That was her name. Corliss had fended me off, laughing. She said, "What you need is some sleep, mate."

I grabbed her and tried to kiss her. Still laughing, she parked me in a chair and stepped into the bathroom to change into a negligee. Then, while she was undressing, we went through the same routine that I had just gone through with Mamie. Almost verbatim.

I called into the bathroom that she was very pretty.

"Thank you," she called back. "Just get paid off, mate?"

"This morning."

"You mean yesterday morning."

"That's right."

"Long trip?"

"Three years."

"No ports?"

"None as nice as this one."

It was a thirsty business, waiting. I remember wishing I'd brought a bottle with me. Then Corliss came out of the bathroom, wearing a clinging white silk negligee. Her loveliness was a flame reaching out and burning me.

I got to my feet and leaned against the wall by the bed to keep the cottage from capsizing. The floor was beginning to heave. Corliss floated always just out of my reach.

"How much money do you have, sailor?" she asked me.

Drunk as I was, I played it cagey. I was still going home to Hibbing. I was still going to buy a farm. I pulled a handful of the crap-game money from my pocket. "Plenty, baby," I told her.

I flopped down on the bed and patted it. "Come on, baby," I said. "Remember I've been at sea three years."

Corliss smiled at me, amused. "Let's have a drink first," she suggested.

She reached on a shelf for a bottle. As she lifted her arm, her robe gaped. My breathing almost choked me. I *had* to have her. I meant to. I'd never seen anyone so lovely.

She wasn't more than twenty-three or twenty-four. Her hair was the color of honey. Her eyes and quarter-inch lashes were brown. She didn't weigh a hundred pounds stripped, but her hips and breasts were exquisitely molded.

She floated toward me with the bottle in one hand and a water glass in the other. I reached out and caught my fingers in the neck of the white negligee.

She filled the glass three-fourths full of rum. "Here. Drink this first."

I sipped the rum, pulling her toward me. She put the bottle on the deck, patted my hand, and sat on the bed beside me, smiling. "I'm awfully sorry, but you're in for a sad awakening, mate."

I reversed my hand. The skin on her stomach was soft and silky.

She took my hand away. "Don't. What you need is some sleep."

I finished the rum in the glass. "And then?"

"And then," she said, "we'll see. What's your name, mate?"

I told her. "Swen. But everyone calls me Swede."

She laughed, and it sounded like the tinkling of glass bangles in the doorway of a Chinese shop. "I wonder why."

Her robe had gaped open again. When she laughed I could see her muscles ripple. I put my hand on her leg

17

this time. She liked it. I could tell. The muscles in her leg twitched spasmodically. Then she pushed my hand away. Her eyes filled with tears.

"What's the idea?" I asked her.

She said, "I wish I were what you think I am. But it so happens that I'm not. So—sorry, Swede. All you get is a cottage and some shut-eye. I have to have love with mine."

I pushed her back on the bed and pressed my face against hers. "Don't give me that."

Corliss clung to me, quivering, demanding. But only for a moment. Then all her fire was gone. Even her flesh felt different. I'd hooked one finger in her bra and ripped it. Her breasts were cold white marble.

"Don't," she said sharply. "Don't."

I laughed and kissed her again. Then, moaning, she picked the rum bottle from the deck and smashed it over my head and both of us were standing in the middle of the room, rum mixed with blood on my face, the little blonde panting:

"I warned you."

She had blood on her, too. My blood. My knees were rubber. I was out on a stormy sea in the dead eye of a calm with the start of a nasty roll making. One eye was blinded with blood. I clung to the rail of the bridge to keep from going over.

Then Corliss was on the bridge with me, pressing herself against me, holding me up.

"Oh, God," she whimpered, "I'm sorry."

Then a big green wave had swept over the bridge and carried me down and down into the cool black depths.

I sat on the bed feeling cheated. I'd made a fool of myself for nothing. The little blonde had been clever. She'd clipped me for my entire roll and hadn't bothered to try to earn her money. As if any dame was worth fifteen thousand dollars.

Boy. Would Ginty laugh. "Back for a job, eh?" he'd roar, his fat beer belly bobbling. "I thought you were quitting the sea, Swede. I thought you were going back to Minnesota and buy a farm and get married and settle down."

Then he'd give me some goddamn guano run. Or maybe a nitrate freighter. Just to teach me a lesson.

The more I thought, the madder I got. It had taken me three years to save twelve thousand dollars. Now the little blonde had my dough. And all I'd got out of it was a night's lodging. In a single bed. Alone.

The little brunette had known her. They should know her last name at the bar. Also where I could find Corliss. I wanted my money back. I meant to have it. If I had to wreck the joint.

There was a handful of silver on the dresser. I dressed and put it in my pocket. Then I crossed the drive to the bar, the big purple neon parrot watching me.

The bar part of the restaurant was small but expensive-looking, with big white leather booths against the wall. The fat barman looked vaguely familiar.

I laid a silver dollar on the bar. "Bacardi. Light. A double."

He served me without comment. I drank it in two gulps and pushed the glass across the wood.

"Let's go again."

I fumbled for more change. The barman shook his head. "Don't bother with the chicken feed. You don't remember me, do you, mate?"

I admitted, "No. I can't say I do."

"I put you to bed," he told me. "After you insulted Miss Mason this morning." He filled my glass and set the bottle beside it. "Go ahead. Drown yourself. Your credit's good. You even got enough in the safe to bury you."

I asked what he meant by that.

He rested his weight on his palms. "You may or may not remember it, mate, but when you make an ass of yourself this morning and Miss Mason is forced to conk you with a bottle, you are carrying almost fifteen thousand dollars. Fourteen thousand, eight hundred and seventy-five, to be exact. And Miss Mason puts it in the safe so some two-year-old kid don't roll you."

It wasn't the setup I'd expected. I felt the back of my ears get hot. "Corliss is Miss Mason?"

The fat barman nodded, keeping his voice down for the benefit of the other patrons. "That's right. She picks you out of a clip joint yesterday morning. Because she can see you're headed for trouble and due to wind up dead broke. She tries to save your dough for you. And how do you repay her? You insult her. That's how." His bulk quivered with indignation. "If it had been me, I'd have thrown you out on the beach and kept the dough. But Miss Mason is a lady. And when she comes back from San Diego she'll give you all your money, minus the rent on the cabin and what you swill at the bar."

I felt even more of a fool. "Miss Mason lives at the Purple Parrot?"

The barman hooted. "Lives here? She owns it, sailor. Lock, stock, and all the barrels in the basement."

I looked out the window at the landscaped grounds. The Purple Parrot Court was new. It had twenty units with a private beach. With the bar and restaurant, it was worth possibly two hundred thousand dollars.

The back of my neck got as red as my ears. I had no quarrel with Corliss. She had a quarrel with me. She'd picked me out of a clip joint. She'd saved my money for me. She was a lady, not a tart. And I'd repaid her by trying to force her.

I looked up as two guys walked in the door. There was only one thing they could be. They had the build, the walk, the smell. They glanced around the bar, then stood one on each side of my stool.

"What's the idea?" I asked them.

The older of the pair pushed his Stetson back on his head. "The name is Cooper, son," he told me. "Sheriff Cooper. And it would seem you answer the description of a man we've been looking for all day. Blonde. Six feet two. Two hundred pounds. A seaman. A first mate of Scandinavian ancestry. What's your name, fellow?"

I told him. "Nelson."

"Occupation?"

"Seaman."

"Rating?"

"Mate."

He wasn't a bad joe, for a cop. "You hit a man last night?" he asked.

I said, "I was in a fight. As I recall, some pimp tried to kill me."

The barman's fat face colored. He said, "Please, Sheriff. We try to run a respectable place here. Would you mind talking to Nelson outside? There are ladies and children dining."

There was a murmur of approval from the tourists in the booths along the wall. The old joe looked at me. I got off the stool. I'd caused Miss Mason enough trouble. "Sure. Why not?" I said. I led the way out the door. "Yeah. I hit the guy. As I recall, he came at me with a sap."

The wind had freshened and the night was filled with salt spray and the sound of the sea. On the drive in front of the bar, I asked, "So what's the charge?"

The young cop was nasty about it. "Manslaughter, if he dies."

"I hit him that hard?"

"You did."

"Who signed the complaint?"

"His girl," Cooper's deputy said.

I remembered her vaguely. A top-heavy brunette in a faded green dress. With a harsh voice. Shrilling, "Kill the big Swede, Tony!"

I lighted a cigarette, cupping the match against the wind. "So?"

"So what?" Sheriff Cooper asked me.

"What happens now?"

"We talk to the judge," he told me.

Chapter Three

The J.P.'s name was Farrell. Cooper had to dig him out of a poker game in the back room of the Elk's Club. He held the hearing in the Sheriff's office at the Palm Grove brig. It wasn't much of a hearing.

"How you plead, sailor?" he asked me.

I said, "Self-defense. The guy come at me with a sap. I hit him."

"During a crap game?"

"That's right."

Farrell spat tobacco juice over his shoulder. Out an open window. Up against the bole of a palm tree. "How about witnesses, sailor? Who saw him swing this sap?"

I said, "Two avocado ranchers, some construction stiffs back from Guam. Maybe the barman. Although he wasn't in the game."

"You know their names or where Sheriff Cooper can contact them?"

I shook my head. "Not me. The barman's name was Jerry. But I haven't the least idea who the other fellows were. They were just guys I met in a bar."

The J.P. looked at Cooper. "Nelson give you any trouble, Sheriff?"

"Not a bit," Cooper admitted.

Farrell looked back at me. "I'm sorry, Nelson," he said. The little guy sounded as if he meant it. "We've had trouble with Tony before. But the law gives me no leeway. I'll have to bind you over for trial. Your bail will be five hundred dollars."

I asked Sheriff Cooper if I could call the Purple Parrot. He said I could. The fat barman answered the phone.

"The Purple Parrot Bar and Court. Wally speaking."

I asked if Miss Mason had come back from San Diego.

"No. She has not," he told me.

I said, "Well, look. When she does—"

"Yeah?"

"Tell her I'm sorry about last night. And ask her to do me one last favor."

"What?" Wally asked me flatly.

"Ask her to deduct my bill and send someone over to the Palm Grove brig with my money. I'm being held on five hundred dollars' bail."

"For what?"

"For hitting a guy too hard."

He said, "I'll tell her," and hung up.

The deputy's name was Harris. He led me back to a cell and locked me in with two cases of empty Coke bottles, a confiscated four-bit slot machine, some leaky plumbing, and an assortment of curious cockroaches.

For some reason, Harris didn't like me. He smiled nasty at me through the bars. "Let's hope you're not with us long, Nelson. Say, not more than two or three months. Then let's hope that Tony dies."

I asked, "What's eating on you? You getting a cut of the game? Or was he managing your wife?"

His face got red. He started to unlock the door. Then

he changed his mind and strode off down the hall.

The blanket on the cot looked crumby to me. I upended one of the Coke cases and sat with my back against the wall. My headache was gone. I felt fine. It could just be that Corliss would show in person with my money. I hoped so. I wanted to thank her for what she'd done, apologize.

I stopped kidding myself. I'd apologize, of course. I'd thank her for what she'd done for me. But what I really wanted was to see her. As I remembered her, she was lovely.

Still, considering the way I'd acted, she'd probably send one of the help.

The smell of the sea was gone now. All I could smell was dust and disinfectant and the cigar Sheriff Cooper was smoking.

I hoped I was satisfied. I was back on course again, in a cell. The cells I'd sat in. In Mexico, India, China. For brawling, wenching, getting drunk. It was time I settled down, made something of my life. I meant to. When I got out of this mess I'd head straight back for Hibbing. Without taking a single drink. I'd buy a farm. A good one. I'd marry one of the local girls and raise a family.

I lighted a cigarette, thinking. I'd been thirty-three on my last birthday. I wasn't a kid any more. The rolling-stone gag was fact. I'd done a lot of things. And I still didn't amount to a damn. I'd hunted diamonds in Africa. I'd used a machine gun for pay. I had my master's papers in steam for a vessel of any tonnage. And where was I? In a cell in a hick-town brig. Lucky I had a dime. The little blonde was one dame in a thousand. If it hadn't been for her, I'd be lying in some gutter, broke.

There were two four-bit pieces in my silver. I dropped one in the slot machine and pulled the lever. Two plums and a lemon came up. That for you, sailor. Phooey.

I sat back on the Coke case, thinking of Corliss.

"I wish I were what you think I am," she'd told me. With tears in her eyes. "But I have to have love with mine."

Love? I had plenty of love.

She'd wanted me plenty bad, too. Her flesh had crawled under my fingers. I began to sweat, remembering. Wanting what I'd seen. So she owned a tourist court. So what?

I got up and paced the cell, two steps forward, two back, while my mind and imagination squirreled across the steel mesh.

"I have to have love with mine."

To keep from blowing my top, I dropped the other four-bit piece in the machine and yanked the lever. Hard. Three bars came up. One right after the other. Snicking into place without any hesitation. Win, place, and show, across the board. Then the trap door of the jackpot tripped and the machine spat half dollars all over the floor in a tinkling of silver; forty or fifty dollars' worth of that beautiful stuff.

An omen?

Out in the office, Sheriff Cooper laughed. "There's a sailor for you."

Harris said, "God damn," and strode back down the hall. His face pressed to the bars, he scowled. "Hey. You can't do that. It's illegal."

"So's adultery," I pointed out. "But they tell me it happens all the time."

I was still picking up half dollars when a car, traveling fast, stopped short in front of the substation. A moment later high heels clicked across cement. I knew who it was before she spoke.

"I beg your pardon," the little blonde said to Sheriff Cooper, "but might I please see Mr. Nelson? I've brought the money for his bail."

I gave Harris the handful of half dollars I'd gathered. "For your trouble, boy."

He cursed me under his breath. With the bars between us.

Corliss' heels continued to make music, tip-tapping down the hall. She was even lovelier than I remembered. She was wearing yellow now. A sports dress. She was bare-legged, with yellow sandals to match her dress. And a white gardenia in her hair, over a smile for me.

"Hello there, you," she said.

"Hello yourself," I said. "It seems I can't get out of your sight without getting in trouble, eh?"

"So it would seem," she laughed. "I got here as soon as I could. Ninety most of the way. I started as soon as Wally told me."

She put her hands through the bars. I held them while Cooper unlocked the door. Then we walked back to the office together, to sign the bail-bond papers, my hand barely touching her elbow. Corliss didn't have to tell me. I knew. She was as glad to see me as I was to see her. Sometimes it happens like that. She wanted me as badly as I wanted her. Even if I was a big drunken Swede who'd caused her a lot of trouble. Who knew? Maybe she was the dream.

The paper work over, Sheriff Cooper walked out to the car with us. It was a pale green Caddy with the top down. Corliss handed me the keys.

"You drive."

I helped her in. Then I walked around to the other side and slid in back of the wheel.

Cooper leaned on the door of the car, still friendly. "Don't do anything foolish, son," he advised me. "I mean like trying to ship out before your trial."

I promised him I wouldn't.

He grinned. "Like Farrell said, we've had lots of trouble with Tony. And even if he should die, the worst you'll probably get is probation. Meanwhile, I'll sniff around and see if I can't locate the two ranchers you say witnessed the fight."

Corliss leaned across me to talk to him, her breasts boring into my arm. "You do that, Sheriff Cooper. Please."

Harris gave me a dirty look.

I turned the motor over and drove north on U.S. 101. "How come?" I asked Corliss.

"How come what?" she asked.

"You came yourself," I said.

She glanced sideways at me. "It could be I wanted to." Her fingers tiptoed down my arm to my hand, leaving little patches of heat behind them the size of her fingertips. "Would you rather I'd sent Wally?"

"No," I admitted. "I wouldn't. And about last night. That is, I mean this morning."

"Yes?"

"I'm sorry."

Corliss laughed her tinkling laugh again. "How many times have you said that in your life, Swen?"

"Not very often," I admitted.

Corliss patted the back of my hand. "I didn't think so. Forget it. Please. It—was partly my fault. I shouldn't have changed into a negligee. I didn't think. I didn't stop to realize—"

"What?"

"That you were as high as you were. That you'd been at sea for three years. Where were you headed, Swen, when you stopped in that awful place?"

"Hibbing, Minnesota."

"Why?"

"To buy a farm."

"You originally came from there?"

"Yeah. A long time ago," I told her.

She was silent for a mile.

"Why so quiet?" I asked.

Corliss wrinkled her nose at me. "I just was thinking."

"Thinking what?"

"How nice it would be."

"What would be nice?"

"To live on a farm."

I glanced sideways at her to see if she was kidding. She didn't seem to be. I felt my way. "Who pressed my uniform and washed my shirt?"

She said, "I did. Why?"

"Because that's the first time that ever happened to me. Because only a woman who likes a man would do a thing like that."

Corliss' voice was small. "Well, maybe I like you."

"How much?"

"A lot."

"At first sight? Roaring drunk, insulting? Treating you like you were a cheap pickup?"

"Maybe I could see the man in back of the rum."

I gripped the wheel of the car hard to keep from pulling over on the shoulder of the road and acting juvenile.

Corliss sensed the strain in me. "Let's not go right back to the court, Swen. Let's find a turnoff somewhere and talk. If I'm right about this thing, we've a lot to talk about."

I began looking for a turnoff.

Her fingers closed on my forearm. "Only promise me one thing."

I said, "Anything." I meant it.

"Please, don't make me hate you, Swen. Don't spoil something that may be very beautiful for both of us by acting like you did this morning." She said it flatly. "I have a distinct aversion to being forced. When I go to bed with you, if I do, this time it's for keeps."

I looked sideways at her. "This time?"

Corliss met my eyes. "I don't claim to be a virgin. Very few young widows are."

Chapter Four

Hitting the jackpot had been an omen. A good one. I laughed and it came out husky. "Maybe I'd better stop and get a bottle of rum. Just in case. Then you can use it if you have to."

She had a deep laugh for a woman. When she really laughed. Starting deep down in her pretty, concave belly. It made her breasts rise and fall.

"That won't be necessary," Corliss said. "I came prepared." She opened the glove compartment and took out a fifth of Bacardi. "I brought my own bottle with me." She was cute as hell about it. "How about a drink, mate?"

I pulled over on the shoulder of the road and had a drink, a big one. From the neck of the bottle. Corliss drank with me. Smiling. Barely wetting her lips. Then I drove on slowly, the bottle on the seat between us, my heart pounding against my ribs, looking for a turnoff.

I found one a quarter mile down the road and followed it to the crest of a high bluff overlooking the sea, with a silver moon laying a course along the thirty-fourth parallel for China.

Down below us, three hundred feet or more, at the base of a sheer cliff, the pound of the swells broke against rock. The wind was heavy with salt spray, and cold. Corliss ran her hands over her bare arms and made a small sound of discomfort. I asked her if she wanted my coat.

"No, thank you, Swen," she said.

She pushed a button and the top came up automatically. Another button closed the windows. I could still hear the sea, but the shutting out of the wind emphasized the smell of her. I liked it.

Corliss lighted a cigarette. "You're wondering about me, aren't you, Swen? You've logged something new this trip."

I sat, afraid to touch her. "That's right."

She blew a small cloud of smoke in my face. "How long have you been at sea?"

"Off and on since I was fifteen."

"And you've known a lot of tramps, haven't you?"

"One way or another. Not all of them wanted money."

I'd left the motor idling and the dash lights on. So I could see her face. Corliss' brown eyes appraised me in the half-dark.

"No. Not from you. It's a wonder they didn't offer to pay you. But even when their love was not for sale, these other women you have known, they were breaking their marriage vows, making a fool of some trusting man who loved them. Right?"

I said, "That would seem to sum it up." The pressure of her thigh was setting me on fire. I lowered the window on my side a little.

"Didn't you ever meet any of the other kind?"

I grinned at her. "There is another kind?"

Corliss slapped me. Lightly. A caress. Her fingers lingering. "Egotist. I'll bet you never heard the fable of the king and the two couriers."

I couldn't take too much of this. I drank from the neck

of the bottle, using the rum as insecticide, to drown the butterflies in my stomach. "No. I can't say that I have."

She told the story well. It was about a king who sent one courier to look for weeds, another to look for flowers. The moral was that each found what he was looking for.

Corliss' fingers fondled the lobe of the ear nearest her. "I wanted you this morning, Swen. Terribly. I fell in love with you on sight. Roaring drunk, filthy, elemental. No half measures. Everyone either a friend or an enemy. I caught on fire when you touched me. It would have been so much easier to pretend I was what you thought I was and let you—well, do what you wanted to do."

"Why didn't you?"

"If I had, we wouldn't be sitting here now."

"Why not?"

"Because I'd never have wanted to see you again. Because I'd have broken my code, allowed myself to be cheap. I meant it. I have to have love, and respect." She sounded worried. "You aren't married, are you, Swede?"

I grinned at her. "That's why I was headed for Hibbing."

"To get married?"

"That was the general idea."

"You have a girl there?"

"No."

"You do have a family, though?"

"A sister."

"In Hibbing?"

"No. I haven't the least idea where she is. We haven't kept in touch for years. And you?"

Corliss sounded puzzled. "What do you mean, and me?"

"Your background, please." Not that I gave a damn. The palms of my hands were wet with sweat. I wiped them on my trousers.

Corliss puffed her cigarette to a glow. "Very ordinary. Outside of the money angle. I, too, was born in a small town. Married at seventeen. To a rich man's son. A lieutenant commander of a submarine." Her eyes glowed in the half-dark. "Jack was a swell guy, Swen. You'd have liked him."

I sat, still afraid to move; the smell of her caught in the hairs in my nose. What the hell did I care about the guy she had been married to? He was dead. He had to be, if she was a widow.

Corliss cried a little. "He was—lost at sea." She looked at the spray-smeared windshield. "He's out there, somewhere."

I gave her a clean handkerchief and took her cigarette away before it burned her fingers. "Here. Make like a foghorn. Blow."

We sat quiet for a long time. Then she asked what I'd done during the war. I said the war had been over for years. At least, the one she was talking about. And I'd just as soon forget it.

Corliss moved my head from side to side. "Please, Mr. Mate. Don't be cross with me. I like sailors. Remember?"

"Sure. You married one."

Corliss took a deep breath. "He's dead. And you're alive." She laughed in her throat, up from where she lived. "And I'm glad. I've been waiting so long for you, Swede."

She kissed me of her own free will. For the first time.

Intensely. Passion in slow motion, as if she were brushing my lips with poppy petals, petals wet with dew.

The sea was roaring now, inside the car. I took her bare shoulders in my hands and pushed her back against the cushion. "Don't do that if you don't mean it," I warned her.

"I mean it, Swen," she said.

"I told you to call me Swede."

"Swede, then."

I cupped a breast. "Be sure."

Corliss clamped one of her hands on mine, having trouble with her breathing. "I am sure. I knew it the minute I saw you at Jerry's last night. With your cap cocked on the side of your head and a lock of tow hair in one eye."

"Roaring drunk, filthy, elemental?"

She breathed the words against my lips. "Roaring drunk, filthy, elemental."

"A hell-raising first mate on a tramp steamer."

"A man. My man."

Sweat beaded on my temples, on my upper lip. I could feel it trickling down my chest. "You've a hell of a lot more money than I have."

She said, "I don't see where money enters into this."

"What if I decide to buy a farm after all?"

"Then I'll sell the court and go with you."

"To Minnesota?"

"To Timbuktu. If that's where you are."

"You mean that?"

"I never meant anything more."

I kissed the tip of her nose, her eyes, her throat, the

hollow between her breasts. They were no longer cold white marble. Corliss lay, her head thrown back, twisting my hair in her fingers.

Then she pushed me away from her forcibly.

"No. Not here. *Not in a car, Swede.*"

I sounded as if I were shouting at her. I was. "I told you to be sure."

She shouted back at me. "I am sure. But I won't be cheap. Not here, Swede. Please."

"Where then?"

"Anywhere. Why not go back to the Purple Parrot?"

I opened the door of the car and got out. The cold wind felt good on my face. I walked down to the edge of the cliff and looked down at the white water breaking against the jagged rocks three hundred feet below. Then I went back to the car and slid in behind the wheel. It was still an effort to speak calmly. "O.K. That's fine with me," I said.

I reached for the ignition. Corliss stopped me. "One last cigarette."

I lit one and gave it to her. Then I bought myself a drink. It went down smooth, like water.

Corliss' voice was still shaky. "Don't be angry with me, Swede. Please. It's just that I want it to be fine. As fine as I know it can be."

I said, "I'll light a candle."

She laughed from deep down again. "But this is for keeps or not at all. You are willing to marry me, Swede?"

I told her, "Boston."

She asked, "What does that mean?"

"On the level. In any church you name."

"A justice of the peace will do."

"Fine," I said. "Fine. We can get our license tomorrow. But until then?"

Corliss came into my arms again and nibbled at my lower lip. "You'll see," she promised. "Just as soon as we get back to the Purple Parrot."

Chapter Five

Sometime during the day a bee had blown into the car. Warmed by the heat, it crawled up the door on my side and across the dash. Then it began to buzz annoyingly in the lower bevel of the windshield on Corliss' side of the car.

I took her cigarette and puffed at it. "You're not handing me a line?"

She brushed a lock of damp hair from her forehead. "About what?"

"About marrying me? You're willing to marry a man you've only known—" I looked at my watch. It was twelve-five. "Well, not very long."

Corliss ran the tip of her tongue along her upper lip. "Why should you ask such a question? Are you hiding something from me?"

"No."

"Would I know you any better if we were engaged six months?"

I said, "I doubt it. But then there's the Purple Parrot."

"What about it?"

"It's worth a lot of money."

"Yes," Corliss admitted. "It is. Almost two hundred thousand dollars. But I can't see that money enters into this."

I warned her. "I won't be *Mr.* Corliss."

She stroked the sleeve of my coat. "I wouldn't ask such a thing of you, Swede."

I revised my plans. "I'd intended to head for Hibbing. Buy a farm. But the main thing was to settle down. Maybe even raise a family. And I don't see why we can't do that just as well in California as we could in Minnesota."

Corliss laughed. Her laughter tinkling again. "Nor I."

The bee continued to buzz, like the drone of a dentist's drill. Corliss reached out a finger and squashed it. Against the glass. Slowly. The small *plop* of its body filled the car with sound.

"Anyway you're through going to sea, Swede," she said. She wiped her finger on the leather upholstery. Her voice was deep in her throat, and husky. "Well? I thought you wanted me."

"I do."

"Then why are we sitting here?"

I turned the car in a sharp U turn and pointed it south, driving along the sea with the wind blowing sand over the highway, through patches of fog at fifty, eighty, ninety miles an hour. I wove in and out, the tires screaming on the curves. Foolish. Lucky. Both of us laughing like mad.

There was a light in the bar but the neon parrot was turned off. I drove past the court and had to back almost a quarter of a mile, with Corliss laughing at me.

In the carport she put her fingers on my lips. "Now quiet, Swede, please. I don't want Wally or Mamie to know until after we're married."

I kissed her fingers. "Sure." I helped her out of the

car. She came into my arms. We kissed until we were breathless. In silence. "Maybe I'd better go to my cottage first." I whispered.

"No." It was more sound than word, made with her tongue against my lips, using my mouth as a sounding board. Corliss molded her body against mine, so close I could feel every contour and detail. "No."

I cursed her in a whisper. "Damn you."

She pressed even closer. "Why?"

"I love you," I whispered.

"I love you, Swede," she breathed.

Then we walked through the chirp of the crickets and the fragrance of nicotiana, our feet crunching in the gravel, around to her front door.

I opened the screen door. Gently. So the spring wouldn't screech. Corliss dug in her purse for her key. A man on the porch coughed. Softly. Apologetically. So close I could have reached out and touched him. Then the overhead light snicked on.

Wally, the fat barman, still wearing his white mess jacket, was sitting in the glider. With a big account book in his lap, a small adding machine on top of the account book, and a huge spike of receipted bills beside him.

Corliss put the back of her hand to her forehead. "Oh, my God. I forgot. This *is* Wednesday night."

Wally gave me a dirty look. "I've been waiting for an hour." He brightened. "And we did real well this week, too. According to my figures, our gross is up three hundred dollars."

Corliss explained to me. "I always go over the books with Wally on Wednesday nights." She stood, undecided, trembling, disappointed, trying to control her voice, her hands.

Wally stood up smugly, holding the account book and the adding machine, waiting.

Corliss put a small hand in mine. "Well, thanks for bringing me home, Mr. Nelson. And thank you for a pleasant drive."

It was dismissal. For now. I said, "Thank you for getting me out of jail, Miss Mason."

She chanced putting her hand on my arm. I could feel the heat of her fingers through the cloth. "You're staying on at the court, of course, until after the trial?"

"Of course."

She said, "I'm glad."

"And I'll see you—?"

Corliss shook her head in a barely perceptible gesture. "In the morning."

Wally beamed. "A three-hundred increase is good. But maybe next week we'll do even better."

I wanted to slap the smirk off the fat fool's face. Instead, I asked if the bar was still open.

He said, "Until two o'clock, Mr. Nelson. Mamie takes over at midnight on Wednesdays. While Miss Mason and I go over the books."

I took a deep breath. "Good night."

"Good night, Mr. Nelson," Corliss said.

There were three cars in front of the bar, one of them with Illinois license plates. The pretty brunette who'd come into the cottage was working back of the bar. I ordered rum and told her to leave the bottle.

"Just as you say, Mr. Nelson," she said.

Four men were clustered at the far end of the bar, talking in whispers. One of them looked like Jerry, the barman in the joint where I'd clipped the Mexican pimp. I considered asking him if he was Jerry, and if he was, to get in touch with Sheriff Cooper. Then I thought to hell with it. I was too burned to be concerned about anything but Corliss. Wanting her was a physical pain.

The Purple Parrot wasn't so wholesome now. Not with the tourists asleep. I didn't like the looks of the four men at the far end of the bar. I'd met their kind before. In bar-rooms all over the world. All four were strictly on the make, their terse whispers crawling between them like so many sticky-footed cockroaches.

Mamie came back with a plate of sandwiches and set it on the wood in front of me. "Eat these. They'll be good for you, Mr. Nelson."

I smeared a Braunschweiger on rye with mustard. It tasted good. I ate four of the sandwiches on the plate, looking at Mamie. She was as pretty as Corliss and about the same age. But life hadn't been kind to her. The corners of her pretty mouth turned down. Her gestures were quick and birdlike. She acted afraid. Of what?

"What you got against men, baby?" I asked her.

Her smile was enigmatic. "Have I something against men?"

I finished the last of the sandwiches and washed it down with rum. "And how come you warned me this evening not even to stop at the bar?"

"I don't know what you're talking about," she lied. And moved off to fill the glasses of the four whispering men.

I picked up the almost full fifth of rum from the bar

and walked across the highway to the beach.

The sea was restless, churning, throwing up a fringe of white spume on the beach, like lace on the bottom of a woman's panties. The sea. The biggest tease of them all. Promising everything, giving nothing. With a million lovers. Including me. I would be glad to be rid of her.

I sat on the sand and drank from the neck of the bottle.

In the morning, Corliss had said. Maybe after we'd got our license in Dago. A hotel. A motel. Anywhere. In the best suite in the best hotel in San Diego. Swede and the future Mrs. Nelson. Or maybe we'd drive up to Los Angeles. And afterward we'd lie in the sun and laugh. Between kisses. We'd laugh and laugh and laugh. Because we'd found each other.

I drank, wondering what marriage would be like, thinking of the responsibility I was taking on. This wasn't a tumble in a hotel room. This was it. For keeps. And such a funny way for a man to meet his wife.

Two of the cars in front of the bar pulled away. I sat a long time, until the bottle was empty. Then I threw it into the sea and walked back across the highway.

The Venetian blinds and the door of Corliss' cottage were closed. She sounded as if she were crying. Or maybe it was only the wind. I considered knocking on her door. But she'd told me:

"Now quiet, Swede, please. I don't want Wally or Mamie to know until after we're married."

The wind tugged my cap from my head. I picked it up and walked on, weaving slightly, feeling like a fool. Corliss would laugh when I told her in the morning.

. Mamie, or someone, had made my bed. I took off my coat and shoes and lay down, riding a gentle swell, feeling good, wishing I had another bottle.

The moonlight shining through the blinds formed silver bars. I hoped marriage wouldn't be like that. I hoped I wasn't making a mistake. But how could I make a mistake with Corliss?

I lay listening to the sea, smelling the nicotiana, remembering the men in the bar, wondering if one of them was Jerry, trying to identify a small sound buzzing through my brain.

Then I realized what it was: a soft squashing sound, a small *plop*.

I wished Corliss hadn't killed the bee. At least, not the way she had. Slowly. Without compunction. Seeming to enjoy what she was doing.

Chapter Six

I dreamed a woman was crying. Then I wasn't so certain I was dreaming. I sat up and turned on the light. Corliss was sitting in the easy chair by the bed, crying softly to herself, as if her heart would break with her next breath.

One of her eyes was swollen shut. She was still wearing the yellow dress, but both the skirt and the bodice of it were shredded.

I said, "For God's sake, what happened to you?"

She continued to sob.

I looked at my watch. I'd been asleep an hour. I got to my feet, with a fifth of rum in me, still plenty drunk. "I asked what happened to you."

Corliss continued to cry in detached sobs. Each sob a ripping sound. As if it were torn out of her chest. Then she began to rock in the chair. "Oh, my God. Oh, my God. Oh, my God."

I knelt beside her. "Honey—"

She pushed me away from her. Agonized. "No. Please. Don't touch me. I—I thought it was Wally, come back for something he'd forgotten. That's why I opened the door. Then he—he—he—"

She screwed up her face to scream. I slapped her, hard. Then I tried to hold her, to keep her from trembling. Corliss twisted away from me. Her face wasn't pretty any more.

"No. Don't touch me," she sobbed. "I don't want any man to ever touch me again."

I got a glass of water from the bathroom. She drank it, gagging and coughing, spitting it all over me. Then she began to rock again.

I knelt beside her. "You mean someone—?"

She nodded, her mouth twisted in a bitter crimson smear. "Jerry. That awful barman from the Beachcomber. Where I met you. I thought it was Wally coming back. I—I unlocked the door and let him in. Then he—he—he—"

I didn't recognize my voice. "He what?"

Corliss, got to her feet. She shouted the words in a whisper. "What do you think? He did it to me twice." She sank back in the chair and began to sob again. "In my own bed."

I staggered away from her into the head and was sick. When I came out I'd never been more sober.

"Why didn't you scream for me?"

She made a hopeless gesture with one hand. "What good would that have done? You were drunk."

"For Wally, then?"

"He had a gun. He said he'd kill me if I screamed." Corliss stopped sobbing and looked at me, through tears. "Do you know what it's like? Do you know what it means to a woman to be forced against her will? Do you know what she goes through mentally and physically?"

I said, "For God's sake, Corliss. Please."

She continued to whip at me. "No. You're a man. You can't know. You can't realize the shame, the utter degradation." Corliss struck out blindly. "You're beasts. All of you."

I wrapped my arms around her. "Where is he now?"

46

She kicked at my shins. "What do you care? You're just another man."

I slapped her, harder this time. "Where is he?"

She sobbed, "On my bed. Passed out. With his gun under my pillow."

I yanked the screen door open and padded barefooted across the grass to her cottage, Corliss running beside me, trying to cover herself. "What are you going to do, Swede?"

"Kill the sonofabitch," I told her.

The light in her cabin was on. I could see the barman from the Beachcomber through the screen door. He was the same lad I had seen in the bar. He was lying on Corliss' bed, snoring, his clothes piled neatly on a chair, is if they had a right to be there.

I yanked him off the bed, then knocked him to the floor with a hard smash to his mouth that made blood spurt. "This is it, you bastard. Get up and take what's coming to you."

He knelt on all fours, shaking his head like a dog. Then he got to his feet. He was drunk, but not sodden. He acted more as if he was drugged; as if he'd mixed goof balls with his drinks or maybe smoked a few reefers to get up the courage to do what he had done.

He was thinking and moving in slow motion. He looked from me to Corliss. And spat blood in her face. "You bitch," he said thickly. "You would." It was an effort for him to speak coherently. Three of his front teeth were loose, bobbling in bloody froth when he talked.

He sat back on the bed. His right hand slid under the pillow and came out with a .45 Colt automatic. It was an effort for him to lift it. He pointed it at me, while time stood still. "And as for you, you big Swede—"

From behind me, her voice throaty and strained with passion, Corliss said, "Hit him. Hit him, Swede. Hit him as hard as you can."

I hit him. Before he could pull the trigger. Making a hammer of my right hand. Putting all my hate and revulsion behind it. The blow caught him on his left temple. His head plopped like an overripe melon, and the whole left side of his face caved in.

The blow knocked him off the bed to the floor.

Corliss opened her mouth as if she were going to scream, then closed it. A peculiar look came into her face. Her upper lip curled away from her teeth.

"You've killed him, Swede."

I stood breathing as if I'd run a long way, sweat beading in the hair on my chest, trickling down. I rubbed my right hand with my left. One of my knuckles was broken. "Yeah. I've killed him."

Corliss opened the screen door and looked out at the sleeping court. None of the lights in the cabins had come on. She closed the screen, then shut the inner door and leaned against it. She was breathing as hard as I was.

"He's dead. Jerry's dead," she panted.

I could smell her across the room.

"Yeah. He's dead."

"You're sure?"

"I'm sure."

She said, "I'm glad. He got what he had coming to him. But what are we going to do, Swede? I mean about him."

My knees gave out, suddenly. I sat on the arm of a

chair, a lump of ice forming in my stomach, trying not to look at the man on the floor.

"There's only one thing we can do."

"What?"

I told her. "Call Sheriff Cooper. Explain just how it happened."

She screamed the words at me in a whisper. "And you think that he'll believe us?"

"Why shouldn't he?"

"He's the law. He's trained to be suspicious. You're already out on bail. For having hit another man too hard."

It was hot in the cottage with the door closed. My whole body was drenched with sweat. I missed the smell of the flowers. I missed the cool swish of the sea.

Corliss left the door and reached up on a high shelf for a partly filled bottle of rye. Her torn dress gaped as she stood on tiptoe.

"You want a drink, Swede?" she asked me.

I shook my head at her. "No."

"You're sure you don't need one?"

"I'm sure."

She put the bottle back on the shelf. "Oh, Swede. This *would* happen now. What *are* we going to do?"

My throat was a vise, squeezing the words. "I told you."

"You mean call Sheriff Cooper?"

"Yes."

Corliss crossed the room and stood in front of me. "No."

"Why not?"

Her voice was fierce. "Because he won't believe me. He won't believe us. He'll take you away from me and lock you up."

My throat continued to strangle my voice. "So what have you to lose? I'm a man, remember?"

Corliss moved in closer and pressed herself against me. I stopped trying not to look at the man on the floor and tried not to look at the breast peeping from her torn dress. In agony. Wondering how low a man could get. Wanting her as I'd never wanted any other woman. After she'd just been forced to lie with another man, and I'd killed the man who had done it.

"Go away. Please," I begged her.

She said, "You're bitter, Swede."

"Why shouldn't I be?"

She pleaded with me. "But you mustn't be, darling. Please. I was excited before. Ashamed." Corliss cupped my face in her hands. "We have our whole lives ahead of us."

"After this?"

"Yes. Even after this."

I slid over the arm onto the seat of the chair to get away from her, to keep from making Corliss hate me for life, with a dead man for witness.

"Get me a cigarette. Please."

Corliss found a pack on the dresser. She lighted a cigarette, then sat in my lap to share it, the soft warm pressure of her body adding to my torture. She knew, she had to know, she couldn't help but know what I was going through.

She sucked the cigarette to a glow, then put it between

my lips. Her words and her thinking were staccato. "No, I've made up my mind."

"About what?"

"About us." Her body seemed stroked by some inner fire. "We can't go to the law. We *can't*. You hear me, Swede?"

I said, "Why can't we go to the law?"

Corliss cupped my face in her hands again and kissed me. For a long time. It was a sweet kiss, without passion but filled with promise. "Because I love you, Swede," she said finally. "Because even after what has happened, I want you, physically, every bit as badly as you want me. Because we aren't going to let this ruin our lives. Because we're going to get married in the morning just exactly as we planned."

I tightened my arms around her waist. "But, Corliss—"

"Yes?"

"Maybe Cooper will understand. After all, there's a law against what Jerry did."

Corliss took the cigarette from my fingers and puffed on it. The light went out of her eyes. "Can you prove that he did it?"

"What do you mean by that?"

"Just exactly what I said." She spaced her words. "Can you prove it?"

"No," I admitted. "But—"

Her laugh was short and bitter. "Can I prove it? No. It's my word against a dead man." She began to cry again. "I know what Sheriff Cooper will think." She made a little short-armed gesture of distaste. "And Harris, that dirty-minded deputy of his. Every time he comes here he feels me with his eyes, doing with his mind what Jerry did with his body."

Her reasoning seemed twisted somehow. But it was difficult for me to think coherently. I wished I'd accepted the drink Corliss had offered me. "What will they think?"

Her swollen left eye was completely closed now. Closed too tight to let tears escape. "They'll think I was being bad with Jerry. And you caught us. They'll think you fought over me."

"But your dress?"

"Anyone can tear a dress," she sobbed. "I could have torn it myself."

"Your eye, then."

Her voice was a little silver hammer pounding at me. "You could have hit me as well as Jerry."

That much was true. I thought a moment. "But if we don't go to the law, what can we do?"

Corliss looked at the man on the floor without pity, the way she had looked at the bee in the car. "We can get rid of his body."

"How?"

"Hide it."

Both of us were panting again. I said, "That's easier said than done. Where would we hide it?"

"In one of the caves."

"What caves?"

"In the mountains above Malibu."

I shook my head. "That's out."

"Why?" she demanded.

I told her. "Because bodies in caves are always found."

Corliss got off my lap and paced the floor like a tawny

caged cat. "Then somewhere else. Figure out something." She threw the words at me. "You're the man I love. You say that you love me."

The cigarette was burning my fingers. I snuffed it out. "I do."

Corliss stopped pacing and faced me. "Then do something about it. Do you *want* to go to jail? Do you prefer that to marrying me?"

I caught at her hips with both hands and tried to pull her to me. "You know better than that."

Corliss twisted her hips free, leaving only the feel of her in my hands.

"Then *think*, Swede." She screamed the words at me. "For both our sakes."

"How well did you know him?" I asked.

She looked at the man on the floor with revulsion. "I didn't know him. I went out with him once. To a Damon Runyon Cancer Fund dance in Manhattan Beach. On the way home he tried to get fresh, do what he did tonight. And I told him that I never wanted to see him again."

"Then what were you doing in his bar last night when you met me?"

"Telling him off," Corliss said. "To get even with me for turning him down, he's been telling it all up and down the beach that I—well, that I'm not the sort of person I ought to be."

"What's his last name?" I asked her.

Corliss said, "Wolkowysk."

"He owned his own bar?"

"I don't know. He claimed that he did. But I doubt it. Why?"

I said, "I'm just wondering how soon he'll be missed."

She lifted her hair away from the back of her neck, then let it drop back in place, like a golden helmet. "*Think,* Swede, please," she begged me. "I—I don't want either of us to go to jail."

"There's no reason why you should," I pointed out. "You'd have been justified in shooting him. Besides, you didn't kill him. I did."

She said, "In the eyes of the law, both of us are equally guilty." Corliss came back into my hands again. "We didn't mean this to happen, did we, Swede?"

"No."

"But it has." Corliss took my palms from her hips and pressed them against her thighs. "Think, darling. At the best this is manslaughter. And even if I go free it could mean a ten-, perhaps a twenty-year sentence for you; locked away in a cell, kissing me once a month through a screen on visiting days. Both of us slowly going mad. Then there's another thing, Swede."

"What's that?"

Her voice was so low I had to lean forward to hear her. "You ought to know. Do I look like the kind of girl who would enjoy going into court and standing before a jury of twelve men and a judge, all of them smirking at me, undressing me with their eyes, thinking nasty thoughts? Do I? Do you think I would enjoy admitting, 'Yes. Jerry Wolkowysk forced me into bed with him. My own bed. At the point of a gun. The night before I was going to be married.' " She flung my hands away, screaming the two words. "*Do I?*"

I got up and walked across the room. I took the bottle

from the shelf and let rye gurgle down my throat. "All right. That does it."

"Does what?"

"We won't call Sheriff Cooper. We'll get rid of the body."

"Where?"

I tilted the bottle again. Whisky dribbled off my chin onto my chest. I mixed it in with the sweat and hair, rubbing it with my fingers. "I don't know. But get dressed and be ready to go. Meanwhile I'll think of something."

Corliss buried her face in her hands.

I opened the door and crossed the grass to my cottage, through the *re-teat, re-teat* of the crickets and the funereal smell of the flowers. I had trouble putting on my shoes and shirt and coat. I wasn't as sober as I'd thought I was. I was glad I wasn't. Regardless of what I did with the body, it was going to be a nasty business.

As I put on my coat, my wallet fell out of my pocket, and with it the bus ticket to Hibbing.

I looked at the ticket for a long time. Then I went back to take care of Wolkowysk.

Chapter Seven

Corliss was standing in front of her dressing table, giving her hair and make-up a quick once-over, trying to hide the swelling under her eye with face powder.

I said, "Never mind your eye. Get dressed."

She said, "Yes, Swede," meekly, and slipped out of her torn yellow dress. There was nothing under it but her. Long hours in the hot Southern California sun had tanned her legs and back a rich copper. But as she padded across the floor to the clothes closet it looked as if she were wearing white satin briefs.

She took a pale green dress from the closet and, holding it in front of her, she crossed the room and kissed me. "I love you, Swede."

"I love you, Corliss," I told her.

We kissed for a long time, straining against each other.

Then I rolled Wolkowysk in the white pile rug on which he'd died. I had to unroll him again, gagging and fighting for breath, when I remembered that his clothes were lying on the chair beside the bed.

Corliss tried to help dress him and couldn't. Her hands shook too badly. She said, "Just the feel of his flesh makes me sick."

I told her to sit on the bed while I dressed him. She sat on a chair instead, watching me with brooding eyes.

I put on his socks and his underwear. I zipped up his

pants. I forced his arms into his shirt and coat. I tied his tie. Handling his body revolted me as much as it did Corliss. But for a different reason.

So he was only a dead man. I'd handled lots of dead men. In Africa. In Central and South America. At sea. But this dead man was different. Wolkowysk was my baby. This one was charged to me. So far it was only manslaughter. But once I dumped his body, no one would believe our story. It was up to me to do a good job of hiding him. For my own sake. If and when his body was found, the tab would read first degree.

When I had him dressed I went to the head and lost the rye. Then I rolled him in the white rug again, being careful to wad most of it around his head to keep blood from dripping on the floor while I carried him out the side door opening into the carport and put him in the turtle back of Corliss' green Caddy.

I locked the turtle back and, at Corliss' suggestion, we went over the cottage on our hands and knees, looking for anything of Wolkowysk's I might have missed.

"I'll buy a new rug the first thing in the morning," she said.

I found his gun on the floor and put it in my pocket. Then I found a few spots of blood where he had leaked through the rug.

Corliss got to her feet, tense with strain. "Now what, Swede?"

I told her to wipe the table, the lamp, the doorknob, anything that he might have touched, while I wiped up the blood on the floor with cold water.

I was glad the deck was asphalt tile and heavily waxed.

As far as I could tell, none of the blood had sunk in. When I finished wiping the floor I wrapped the rag I had used with newspaper and put it in my pocket, along with Wolkowysk's gun.

My shoes squished when I walked. My heavy uniform coat was as wet as if I'd swum a mile in it.

Corliss was as nervous as I was. She tried twice to fasten the straps of her silver sandals. I finally had to fasten them for her. She caught her fingers in my hair and pushed my head back. "Have you thought of anything, Swede? I mean, about him?"

"No," I admitted. "I haven't. How clean are we to start with?"

"What do you mean by that?"

"Did anyone see him come in here?"

Corliss' fingers tightened in my hair. "No. At least, I don't think so."

I stood up and gripped her shoulders. "Be positive."

"I am. Wally had been gone a good five minutes when I heard the knock on the door. I thought it was Wally coming back. That's why I unlocked the door." Her face screwed up as if she were going to scream. "Then he—"

I shook her until her head bobbled. "Stop it. It's over. He's dead. Forget it."

Corliss' fingernails bit into my forearms. "I'll try. Honest I will, Swede."

"What time was it when he came in?"

"I'd say half past two."

"The bar was open or closed?"

"It should have been closed a half hour. Mamie always closes it promptly. She doesn't like to work back of the bar."

"What's her last name?"

"Meek. She manages the court for me. Her husband is the gardener."

"A little man in blue dungarees and a gray sweater?"

"That would describe him. But why the interest in the Meeks?"

I said, "I'm just trying to cover all the angles. Mamie was in the bar tonight. So was Wolkowysk. Would he be apt to confide in her that he was going to call on you?"

Corliss shook her head. "No. I only went out with Jerry the one time. Mamie wouldn't know him from any other customer in the bar."

I got her a camel's-hair coat from the closet and walked her out to the green Cadillac. Then I eased out of the carport as quietly as I could and pointed the car north on U.S. 101, a vague plan forming in my mind. I drove for perhaps five miles, neither of us speaking, being careful to observe the legal maximum. Then I thought of something I should have remembered and jammed on the brakes so hard that a big Diesel trailer almost rammed us.

Corliss caught at my arm. "Now what?"

I gasped, "His car. It's a cinch Wolkowysk didn't walk from Laguna Beach to the Purple Parrot. His car *has* to be back there."

Fear had numbed her brain. "Back where?"

"In front of the Purple Parrot." I shouted the words at her as I swung the car in a sharp U turn and drove back the five miles we had come at ninety miles an hour, cursing the big Diesel trucks making the night haul up to Los Angeles, their drivers blinking their lights and blasting their horns at me.

There were two cars in front of the dark bar. One was a beaten-up Ford. Corliss said it belonged to Wally. The other was a '47 gray Buick super with the keys in the ignition and a pink registry slip made out to Gerald Wolkowysk in a glassine case on the steering column.

I leaned against the Buick smoking a cigarette, listening to the sounds of the crickets, getting my breath back, letting my idea grow.

Then in a lull between trucks I took Wolkowysk out of the turtle back. I unrolled the rug and put it back in the Caddy for future disposal. I'd caved in the left side of Wolkowysk's head. The right side didn't look too bad. If I pulled his hat over his eyes he could pass for drunk. I put him in the right-hand front seat of the Buick and pulled his hat over his eyes.

Corliss watched me in silence, her breasts rising and falling unnaturally fast.

When I had Wolkowysk arranged to suit me, I motioned her under the wheel of the Caddy. "You drive. Follow me."

She whispered, "Where?"

"To that turnoff where we parked."

She brushed my face with the tips of her fingers. "Whatever you say, Swede."

I slid behind the wheel of the Buick and eased it out onto the highway, back the way we had come, driving slowly now, making certain I dimmed my lights for every approaching car and observing what few stop signs there were. I didn't want to be picked up for a traffic violation. Not with the cargo I was carrying.

There was little traffic on the road. Nothing but

trucks rolling north to L.A. and others rolling south to Dago, plus a few early-rising fishermen. Nearing the turnoff I slowed still more. When I reached it I turned off my lights. I hoped Corliss would think to do the same. I didn't want any nosy highway cop investigating our headlights. At least, not until I'd got rid of Wolkowysk.

The fog was thicker here. I drove through it slowly toward the top of the cliff and the cluster of wind-distorted trees under which Corliss and I had parked. When I figured I'd gone far enough, I stopped and set the hand brake. Then I got out of the car and paced the distance to the lip of the cliff. It was a little more than two hundred feet across level solid rock.

I stood near the edge and looked down. The drop was as sheer as I remembered it. Three hundred feet down the waves pounded against a confusion of jagged rocks, the white water sucking in and out of the caves that the sea and time had worn in the base of the cliff.

A cold hand touched mine. I jumped. Then I saw it was Corliss. She'd turned off her lights without being told. The Cadillac was parked a short distance back of the Buick. There was no one to hear her, but she whispered, her whisper almost carried away by the wind. "What are you going to do, Swede?"

I said, "I'm not going to do anything. But Wolkowysk got stinking drunk in your bar last night. So drunk he drove his car off a cliff."

Corliss' fingernails dug into my back as she kissed me. Her kiss was a prayer, a wish on a star. "What can I do, Swede?"

I said, "Stand five feet from the edge of the cliff. As close to the path of the car as you dare."

She protested, "But I want to help."

Tension began to build in me like steam in a boiler, until I was afraid I'd blow my top any minute. "You will be helping," I snarled. "When I'm even with you, I'll jump. Take off your coat. That dress will show up better in the fog."

She dropped her coat and stood where I'd told her to stand. I walked back to the Buick, stiff-kneed, wishing that Wolkowysk hadn't been such a cheap sonofabitch. If he'd laid out the extra money for Dynaflow, goosing the car over the cliff would be simple.

Wolkowysk hadn't gone for a walk. His smashed head still lolled on the seat back. I cursed him as I took the newspaper-wrapped rag from my pocket. I threw the paper away and used the rag to wipe my fingerprints off the wheel. When I was certain the wheel was clean I pulled his stiffening body under it and bent his fingers around the wheel.

The fog was thicker now, a wall of gray between me and the lip of the cliff. I hoped I could see Corliss in time to jump. I made certain the car was in neutral. Then I released the emergency brake, turned on the ignition, and stepped on the accelerator.

The car would idle fine. Finding a way to feed it gas was another matter. I solved the problem by wedging Wolkowysk's right foot in such a way that when I pushed on his left shoulder his foot would depress the gas pedal. I tried it a couple of times, making the motor roar, so I could be sure it would work.

My back ached by the time I was set. I wanted a cigarette. I wanted to be anywhere but where I was. But I had to go through with it now. I pushed the left front door open until the catch held it. Then, standing on the sliver of running board on my left foot, my right foot depressing the clutch pedal, I switched on the lights, shifted the car into second gear, took my foot off the clutch, and pushed hard on Wolkowysk's shoulder.

The car darted forward like a startled dolphin sighting a shark, me helping Wolkowysk steer with my left hand. When I saw Corliss I jumped backward, pushing myself away from the car—and almost didn't make it.

As the front wheels went over the edge the pan dropped down on the rock with a scream of tortured metal, teetering the car and springing the left rear door. The door swung forward like a flat pile driver, hitting me in the back as I jumped, slamming me down on the rock at the very lip of the cliff, my legs dangling in space, the big car beside me grinding desperately for life. On the edge of nothing.

There was a screaming in my ears. Hands clawed at me. I realized it was Corliss, tugging me back to safety as the Buick fell end over end, its headlights sweeping the sky as it plunged three hundred feet into jagged rock and white water, carrying Jerry Wolkowysk with it.

I lay on the lip of the cliff, exhausted, fighting for breath. Corliss lay a few feet away. In her struggle to keep me from going over the cliff, the low neckline of her dress had slipped down over one shoulder, half exposing her breast. As I watched her she wriggled across the rock toward me. Corliss pulled the dress still farther down on her shoulder, and her upper lip curled away from her teeth. She looked the way she had in the cabin right after I'd killed Wolkowysk.

She hooked the fingers of my hand in her bodice. "Take it off, Swede," she pleaded. "Help me. Please."

Her dress ripped easily and then she was wriggling out of what was left of the cloth. I felt her eager fingers fumbling at my shirt, my tie. Then her searching mouth found mine as we both lay in the moonlight, her body a fever, a fire, burning wherever her flesh touched me.

Corliss cupped the back of my head in her hands. "They won't ever find him, will they, Swede?"

I kissed her eyes. "I hope not."

She pressed herself against me. "They can't. Not now. It wouldn't be fair." Her hands caressed my shoulders, my back. "I'm safe with you, aren't I, Swede?"

I kissed her hair, her cheeks, her lips. "Of course."

"You love me?"

I lifted my head to look at her. "I do."

Corliss' eyes burned into mine. "I love you, Swede. Say you love me."

"I love you."

She bit my chest. "Then *prove* it," she screamed at me. "*Prove* it."

I did, the hard rock ripping our flesh. We were mad. We had reason to be. We were Adam and Eve dressed in fog, escaping from fear into each other's arms. And to hell with the fiery angel with the flaming sword. It was brutal. Elemental. Good. There was no right. There was no wrong. There was only Corliss and Swede.

When at last I rolled on my elbow and lay breathless,

looking at her, Corliss lay still on her back in the moon-light, her hair a golden pillow, fog eddying over her like a transparent blanket. Her upper lip covered her teeth again. Her half-closed eyes were sullen. The future Mrs. Nelson, I thought, and I wished she had some clothes on.

The wind off the sea was suddenly cold. I could taste salt on my lips. The pound of the waves where the Buick was dying was like the booming of a great drum.

My breath caught in my chest. It was a funny feeling. I tried to brush it aside. I couldn't. It was ridiculous, but I had a feeling that this time, I was the one who had been forced.

Chapter Eight

Neither Corliss nor I spoke on our way back to the Purple Parrot. I ran the green Cadillac into the carport of her cottage. We sat in the dark, still silent. Then Corliss came into my arms.

"I love you, Swede," she said.

"I love you, Corliss," I told her.

She kissed me without heat. "And this won't change the other? We'll be married today?"

I said, "This afternoon."

"Where?"

"In Los Angeles or San Diego. Whichever you prefer."

Corliss thought a moment. "I think I'd like to be married in L.A."

I said, "Los Angeles is fine with me."

She took her keys from her bag and opened the door of the car.

"You'll be all right?" I asked her.

"I—think so," she said.

She turned and kissed me again. With more heat this time. "Thank you, Swede," she said simply. Then, holding her coat together to cover her torn dress, she unlocked the door of her cottage and closed it softly behind her.

I waited until I saw a light. Then I walked next door to Number 3. Sometime toward dawn I slept. But not for long. At seven o'clock there was a loud flurry of talking and laughing and slamming of cottage and car doors in the carport next to my cottage as some cheerful character from Iowa got off to an early start for Tucson.

"Yup. Gonna make four hunnerd an' twenty-two miles t'day," he cackled.

I wished I could have slept. There was a sour taste in my mouth. I wanted a cup of coffee. There was a light in the kitchen of the restaurant, but none in the bar or dining room.

To kill time, I showered and shaved. While I was shaving there was a thud on the door, like the single tap of a knuckle. My nerves still weren't any too steady. I damn near cut myself. I laid down the razor and looked out the window again. It seemed a morning paper was included in the eight dollars' rent per cabin. The nondescript man in blue dungarees and gray sweater was distributing the Los Angeles Times.

I propped my paper behind the faucets and glanced at the front page while I finished shaving. Two of the headlines were new. One of the better-known dewy-eyed movie glamour girls had announced her intention of going to the altar, and presumably to bed, with her fifth husband. A new tax increase had been approved. The rich guy I'd read about the first night of my binge was still on the front page. It was quite a yarn. It seemed he had been the thirty-five-year-old screwball son of a respected and very wealthy old-line Chicago family, with a penchant for getting into messes. His last escapade had been to marry a youthful red-haired South Chicago stripper named—but not called—Sophia Palanka and take her on a grand tour of Europe. The happy bridal pair had cabled from London and Paris, then from Bucharest. And that had been the last that had ever been heard from Phillip E. Palmer III.

In the three intervening years there had been considerable diplomatic exchange about the matter. From time to time, goaded by the playboy's family, the State Department had attempted to make another Vogeler case of his mysterious disappearance. And from time to time the indignant Rumanian authorities had protested they knew anything whatsoever about Phillip E. Palmer III and his slightly tarnished bride.

There the matter had rested until some duck hunters had found a body in a slough near Gary, Indiana, and the body had been identified as that of the missing playboy who was supposed to have disappeared back of the Iron Curtain.

He had been dead a long time—quite possibly for three years. Further checking revealed that shortly before his reported departure for Europe he had cashed in stocks and bonds for a total of a quarter of a million dollars, which same money had disappeared with him.

Now the F.B.I. was inclined to believe he had been murdered shortly after his marriage to Sophia Palanka and the man with whom the red-haired stripper had sailed for Europe had been one Lippy Saltz, a small-time Chicago gambler who bore a superficial resemblance to Palmer. At least enough for passport purposes. The names on the passports had read, of course, Mr. and Mrs. Phillip E. Palmer III.

The red-haired stripper had disappeared as completely as Palmer. The F.B.I., however, had traced Lippy

Saltz as far west as Las Vegas and, according to the lead of the reporter who handled the story, Lippy's apprehension and arrest were expected momentarily.

I washed the lather from my face and looked out the front window again. There was a light in the dining room.

I put on my coat and cap and crossed the drive feeling sorry for Lippy Saltz. I knew how the guy must feel. I'd be looking in the papers, too. From now on. A guy named Jerry Wolkowysk was dead. I'd killed him. The wreckage of his car was certain to be discovered. His body might or might not be found. I wiped sudden sweat from the leather band of my cap. Corliss and I might get away with it. We might not. There were so many little things a man didn't think of at the time. Little things that bobbed up to sink him.

The bar was still closed but the restaurant part was open for business. A heavy-set older woman, wearing a white nylon uniform with a big purple parrot embroidered on one shoulder, was drawing fresh coffee from an urn. Mamie was drinking orange juice at a table by the window.

I drew out a chair and sat across from her. "Hi."

"Hi yourself," she said.

I ordered wheat cakes and eggs and ham. "And my coffee right now, if you please."

"Yes, sir," the waitress said.

I drank my coffee looking at Mamie. I didn't know Meek. I'd only seen him twice, both times at a distance. But unless he had hidden charms, the brunette had fallen on her head when she had married him. With her looks and body, she could have been a lot more choosy.

"Feel better now, sailor?" she asked me.

I asked what she meant by that.

Instead of answering me she said, "I wish I was a man." She finished her toast and wiped her fingers on her napkin. "A man can do so many things. He can go to sea. He can be a soldier. He can fly." Her smile turned wry. "He can crawl in and out of beds. He can get drunk and into messes. Then all he has to do is sober up and take a bath and no one thinks less of him."

"But a woman can't, huh?"

"No."

"Why can't she?"

Mamie lighted a cigarette. "Because she's supposed to be good. She can't be half bad like a man can. With a woman it's all or nothing."

I grinned over my cup at her. "What's the idea so early in the morning, kid? You get out on the wrong side of the bed or something?"

She blew smoke at me. "Maybe even the wrong bed. How would you like to do me a favor, Nelson?"

I said that depended on the favor.

She reached across the table and gripped my wrist. With surprising strength for a woman. "When you finish your breakfast, shove off."

"Why should I?"

"I told you that the first day you made port. I think you're in danger here."

"What sort of danger?"

She shook her head slowly. "I can't tell you that. I don't know. But I can tell from my husband's snide remarks that—"

She stopped it there as the swinging doors into the kitchen opened. Meek didn't look any better close up than he did at a distance. He wasn't as old as I'd judged him to be. He was a man in his middle or late thirties. His hair was beginning to recede. But from the lines stamped in his thin face, I'd say he hadn't thrown anything over his shoulder or poured anything down the drain. He looked at us, clearing his throat.

"Number Fourteen is checking out, Mamie," he said finally.

The brunette opened her mouth to say something, took her hand off my wrist instead, and walked out the door he was holding open for her.

The door swung shut behind them. I looked at my wrist. Mamie's nails had dug into the flesh. The heavy-set waitress brought my breakfast. The food looked good, but my appetite was gone. I was nervous again, jumpy.

It was the second time Mamie had warned me to shove off. Why? It could be she was jealous. Some women are that way. There couldn't be any other reason for her to say what she had. She *couldn't* know about Jerry Wolkowysk. No one knew that. No one but myself and Corliss.

I pushed my food around the plate, then forced myself to eat. Mamie *had* to be jealous. That was all it could be. She was as pretty as Corliss. Her body was just as lovely. But Corliss had everything that any woman could want . while all she had was a job and Meek.

Sweat beaded on my face. Still, Mamie hadn't been out on the cliff. That I knew. All she could possibly know about me and Corliss was that Corliss had brought me to the court to keep me out of trouble; that I had got fresh and Corliss had slugged me with a bottle; that Corliss had brought my money to the Palm Grove brig and we might have parked for an hour or so on our way back to the Purple Parrot. And, possibly, that we had taken an early morning ride together.

I pulled the morning paper Mamie had been reading to my side of the table and ordered another cup of coffee.

"How long has Mrs. Meek managed the court?" I asked the waitress.

"I think almost two years," she told me.

For want of something better to do, I read the Palmer story again. When you got down into the bulk of it, while the F.B.I. might have traced Lippy Saltz as far west as Las Vegas, his imminent apprehension was the reporter's own idea. The F.B.I. wasn't talking. There was only one direct quote. That was a statement by a Chicago agent to the effect that one small mistake on Sophia Palanka's part had given them what pertinent information they had.

One small mistake. That was all it took.

I wondered if I'd made any. I thought of two and really began to sweat.

I'd wiped the wheel of Wolkowysk's car. Then I'd released the hand brake and used my left hand to steer the car to the lip of the cliff. If the car was found and murder was suspected, my fingerprints were on the brake button release and the left half of the wheel. More, the bloody white pile rug on which Wolkowysk had died was still in the back of Corliss' car.

I patted my face with my napkin.

"Hot in the sun, isn't it?" the waitress said pleasantly.

"Yeah. Hot," I agreed.

I couldn't do anything about the fingerprints except hope the rocks and waves would grind the Buick to pieces before it was found. The rug was something else. I had to destroy the rug and buy one to replace it as soon as I possibly could.

I dropped two bills on the table to cover the check and tip and walked out and leaned against Wally the barman's beaten-up Ford.

The wind sweeping across the highway was cool on my face. It felt good. I stood looking at Corliss' carport, wondering how I could get the rug out of the back. I didn't see how I could, at least without someone seeing me. I'd have to dispose of the rug on our way to L.A. to be married. But how? How did a man go about getting rid of a bloody three-by-four loop pile rug?

The little things.

I crossed the highway to the beach and walked down it for a quarter of a mile. Maybe I hadn't been smart in telling Ginty I was washed up with the sea and the line. It took brains to operate a farm. Maybe I wasn't smart enough to make a living on shore.

Hell. I hadn't even been smart enough to get on a bus for Hibbing. On the other hand, if I had, I wouldn't be marrying Corliss.

I walked back down the beach to the Purple Parrot and across the highway to the drive. Corliss' door was still closed. The blinds on her windows were drawn.

I flipped a mental coin trying to decide whether to go back in the bar and see if I could persuade the heavy-set waitress to sell me a couple of drinks before legal opening time, or try to get a few more hours of sleep. I decided to try for sack time.

The screen door of the office was open. I could hear Mamie crying inside. Meek was pruning a climbing rose with a jackknife. As I came abaft he turned and faced me.

"Just a minute, mate."

I stopped and looked at him. "Yes?"

He gripped the jackknife like a dagger. "Look. I know my wife was in your cottage a couple of times the other day. I know you're a big, good-looking joe, the kind dames go for."

"So?" I asked him.

"So keep away from my wife from now on."

I told him the truth. "I haven't the slightest interest in your wife, friend."

His face was blue with cold. He wiped his nose on the sleeve of his sweater. "Sure. That's why you were holding hands in the restaurant just now. So I'm warning you. See? Stay away from Mamie."

I got a little sore. "Or what?"

Meek told me. "Or I'll stick a knife in you."

I doubled my fist to hit him, then unclenched it. He was too little for me to hit. I was apt to crack his head like an eggshell. Like I'd caved in Jerry Wolkowysk's head.

The thought made my breakfast turn over.

"O.K.," I said and walked on.

Chapter Nine

It was ten when Corliss woke up. It was noon by the time she was dressed and ready to leave for L.A. Her eye looked better than it had when I had kissed her good night. It was still badly puffed, but she'd hidden the discoloring with a good cold cream and powder job. Her sunglasses hid it completely, but every time I looked at her eye I felt better about Wolkowysk.

As we pulled away from the court I asked her how she'd slept.

She said, "I didn't sleep at all until I'd taken three seconals." Her lower lip quivered. "It all seems like a bad dream."

I said, "I'm afraid it wasn't. I killed the guy and we dumped him. Now it's fifty-fifty if we beat the law."

Corliss was indignant. "But think what he did! Certainly that's against the law. Certainly I had a right to have my future husband defend me."

I used the lighter to touch off a cigarette and offered her first puff. "I tried to point that out last night. Remember? I wanted to call Sheriff Cooper. But you wanted no part of the law."

Corliss smoked in silence for a mile. Then she moved closer to me on the seat. "I'm sorry, Swede." She sounded like a contrite little girl who'd just kicked her playmate's lollypop into the dust. "I've got you into something awful, haven't I?"

I took the cigarette back. "Anyway, it's done."

I was still keeping my speed down and glancing in the rear-vision mirror from time to time. I didn't want a cop to pick us up before I got rid of the rug.

Corliss laid her hand on my arm. "You still love me? You still want to marry me?"

I patted her hand. "I still love you. I still want to marry you."

Both statements were true. I'd meant what I'd told Ginty. I was through with the sea. I'd spent eighteen years afloat. And what had it got me? Twelve thousand dollars in cash, which I'd been ready to blow on one last binge. A busted nose, broken in a brawl in Port Said over a Berber wench I wouldn't have spat on if I'd been sober. A bedding acquaintance with tarts all over the world. In Lisbon, Suez, and Capetown. In Bremen, in London, Murmansk. In Colón, in Rio, in Lima. In Yokohama, in Macao and Brisbane. Starting from scratch every time I shipped out, while other men my age had homes and families. It was time I sent down roots. It was time I stopped spending life as if it were only money. I realized my breathing was labored. Besides, I wouldn't really feel safe again until Corliss and I were married.

The police could pound on me until both of us were pulp without getting anywhere. I could take it. I knew. I'd been through a lot of fish-bowl sessions. It was different with Corliss. A few hours under the light with smart cops shooting questions at her in relays and she would get hysterical and tell her whole life story. But a wife couldn't be forced to testify against her husband. And Corliss was the only person in the world who *knew*

I'd killed Wolkowysk.

Her fingers bit into my arm. "Are you as frightened as I am, Swede? Do you feel sort of sick to your stomach?"

I nodded. "Yeah."

She looked back at the wicker basket on the jump seat. "Then why did you have Cora prepare a picnic lunch? I can't eat a thing. It would choke me."

I said she'd find out why I'd had the lunch packed in a few minutes, as soon as we came to a suitable stretch of beach. I glanced sideways at her white face. "Now you tell me something, honey. We're in this thing together. We have to be truthful with each other, don't we?"

"Of course."

"Then tell me this. And remember the cops may check and I'll have to know where I stand. How well did you know Jerry?"

Corliss folded her hands in her lap. "I told you last night, Swede."

"Tell me again."

Tears trickled out from under her sunglasses. "I went to one dance with him. In Manhattan Beach. For the Damon Runyon Cancer Fund. I had to fight him all the way home in the car." The tears rolled faster. "Then, to get even with me, he told it all up and down the highway that I was bad. That I'd do it for twenty dollars. So I went to his place to raise hell. And there you were. Drunk, and hurt, and bloody, but grinning at me. And I forgot what I'd gone there for."

I handed her my handkerchief. "O.K. That's fine. Stop crying. Just so I know."

Her voice was small. "Say you believe me."

"I believe you."

I found the kind of beach I wanted just above Oceanside. The highway ran close to the ocean. There wasn't a house for a mile in either direction. I pulled off the highway on the lee shoulder of the road and helped Corliss out of the car. Then I carried the wicker hamper and a blanket to the beach.

I spread the blanket on the sand and told Corliss to set out the lunch I'd had the heavy-set waitress pack. She thrust out her underlip in a sullen pout but did as she was told. While she was spreading the lunch on the blanket I gathered a big pile of driftwood.

The tide was out. I laid my fire well down on the shingle where the incoming tide would cover and dispose of the ashes. When it was burning well I went back to the car for the rug. Before leaving the court I'd soaked it in gasoline, rolled it into a tight bundle, and wrapped it in newspaper. A dozen motorists saw me carry it from the car to the fire.

"What's that?" Corliss asked.

"The rug we wrapped Wolkowysk in."

The color drained from her cheeks. I thought for a minute she was going to faint.

I dropped the rug on the fire. Then I sat down on the blanket beside her and made her take a big drink of the rum-laced coffee in the vacuum bottle. The color came back to her cheeks. She snuggled her hand into mine. I ate a ham sandwich with the other. For the sake of the folks driving by. While we watched the rug burn.

The back of it was rubberized and smelled worse than the cotton, but the wind was blowing offshore. To the folks in the passing cars we were just a sailor and his girl picnicking on a cool day, with a fire to keep us warm.

Back in the car again, Corliss said, "I'm glad you thought of the rug."

I said, "So am I." I wished I could do as much for the wheel of Wolkowysk's car.

The closer we got to L.A., the colder and darker it got. I rolled up the windows and turned on the heater. Corliss rode with her thigh pressed to mine. I could smell the perfume of her hair. It made me think of her hair on the cliff. I began to want her again, driving into Los Angeles through the smog on U.S. 101.

Corliss was as nervous as I was. She picked at the buttons of her coat. She twisted on the seat. I could see her lips move, telling imaginary beads every time we passed a police car.

We came into Anaheim in back of an Ohio car. At the second intersection its driver signaled a right-hand turn from the right-hand lane, then turned left in front of me. I had to stand on the brake to keep from ramming the bastard.

A parked radio car roared off after the foreign license. I drove on, shaken. Corliss began to knead my right thigh in a nervous gesture, setting me on fire.

I snarled at her. "Don't do that."

She spat back, "Why not?"

I said, "Because if you do I'm going to pull over to the curb, and the passers-by will be shocked."

Her lower lip thrust out. "You wouldn't dare."

"If I burn for it," I told her.

She believed me.

I parked in a three-hour zone on Spring Street. Corliss' eyes were still sullen. She said, "We're nowhere near the license bureau."

"First the rings," I told her. "It so happens the Nelsons only marry once, and we always do it right."

The sullen look left her face. Her lower lip quivered as though she were going to cry.

"If you cry I'll slap you," I told her.

Her lower lip continued to quiver. She pressed the back of my hand to her cheek. Her voice was small. "With love. From me to you."

I found a small jewelry store up the block. The lad who owned it took one look at my uniform and, brushing the clerk aside, insisted on waiting on us himself.

"An engagement ring and a wedding band. Right, mate?"

I said, "That's correct. For cash."

He dipped back of the counter and came up with a black plush tray of rings.

The one Corliss said she liked best was eighteen hundred dollars. The wedding band came to three hundred more. It was a trifle too large for Corliss' finger, but she insisted on having it, saying the engagement ring would keep it on.

I counted the cash on the counter, plus the tax, and we were out on Spring Street again, me grinning all over my face. The jeweler had put the rings in small satin-lined white boxes. Out on the walk I took the boxes out of my pocket and reached for Corliss' left hand.

She put her hand behind her. "No. Not now, Swede. Please."

"Then when?"

She said, "When we're married, stupid," then took the sting out of the name by kissing me. "That is, if you still want to marry me."

I made a fist and rolled my knuckles across her thigh. Brutally. Hurting her. Making her wince. So there would be no misunderstanding.

"What do you think?"

Corliss knew what I meant. For a moment Spring Street faded out and we were back on the lip of the cliff in the moonlight and fog with the Buick dying on the rocks beneath us. Her upper lip curled away from her teeth. A strained look came into her eyes. She ran her hands over her breasts as if they hurt her.

"I think we'd better look up the license bureau," she said.

We had to wait in line at the bureau. Corliss gave her name as Mrs. John Mason, twenty-three; occupation, tourist-court owner; married status, widow. I signed on as Swen Nelson, thirty-three; occupation, seaman; unmarried. Both of us white Americans born in the U.S.A.

Then the matter of V.D. clearance came up. The clerk asked for our certificates. I told him we didn't have any. He said he was very sorry, but he couldn't issue a license until we had taken a blood test and suggested we go to one of the laboratories that specialized in giving them. I asked him how long it would take to get a certificate.

He said, "It usually takes three days. But sometimes they come through in two."

Corliss asked, "How about San Diego? Would we have to have a certificate there?"

The clerk said, "It's a state law, miss."

In the hall Corliss thrust out her lip in a sullen pout. "You promised to marry me. Today."

I was as disappointed as she was. I blew my top. "What the hell do you want me to do? Fly up to Sacramento and get a special dispensation from the governor?"

I might have saved my breath. Corliss didn't even hear me. She repeated:

"You promised to marry me. Today. I won't wait three days. I won't."

Her lower lip stopped protruding and quivered. She began to cry without sound.

I could sense hysteria building in her. The last thing I wanted to happen was for her to go to pieces and some bighearted cop to stop and ask what was the matter.

"All right. I'll think of something," I said. "We'll still get married today."

Corliss looked at me suspiciously. "Where?"

I told her the truth. "I don't know."

I walked her out of the building and into the first bar we came to and ordered a double rum for both of us while I considered the situation.

Women.

It seemed inconceivable, but after what had happened on the cliff, our getting married meant more to Corliss than the fact that we might be tagged for killing Jerry Wolkowysk. Now she had given herself to me, she wanted to make it legal. Or maybe she was thinking of Wolkowysk. Maybe she wanted me as tightly bound to her as I wanted her tied to me.

I asked, "Why are you in such a hurry to get married, baby?"

Corliss sipped her rum. Her brown eyes were thoughtful now. "For one thing, I may be pregnant."

"Three days won't make much difference."

"It will to me," she said. She bit at her lower lip. "It could make all the difference in the world."

"You mean that?"

"I do."

It could be so. Some women are that way. I had been told. Corliss wasn't just another tramp. This time it was for keeps. For both of us. And she had wanted it to be beautiful.

I moved over onto the same side of the booth with her. "All right. Let's do this proper. Will you marry me, Corliss?"

She said, "Stop kidding and think."

I said, "I'm not kidding. Will you marry me?"

"When?"

"Today."

"Yes."

I took one of the ring boxes from my pocket and slipped the solitaire on the proper finger. In the light from the lamp in the booth it looked like a two-carat tear, if a tear could catch on fire.

I kissed her finger. Gently. Smiling. With love. "O.K. That's the first step. Now finish your drink and let's go."

Corliss looked from the diamond at me. "Go where?"

I told her. "Tijuana."

Chapter Ten

The traffic on the road was even thicker than it had been. To make time, I cut back through Norfolk and Seal Beach on Alternate 101. After Newport we had clear sailing.

The ocean was a sheet of purple glass without a flaw or ripple in it. Out on the horizon a toy freighter sailed hull down for the Orient. Now and then a hardy bather splintered the edge of the glass nearest the highway, and swam effortlessly away from shore.

Corliss rode with her left hand on my thigh, sitting sideways. Her skirt crawled up over her knees. I could see her tanned thighs over her stockings. I tried not to think of her that way. There was more to marriage than sex. There was love, and trust, and respect. Corliss wanted it to be beautiful. Suddenly, so did I. Love was a will-o'-the-wisp, St. Elmo's fire. A dream I'd stood watch with many times on oceans all over the world. And now it had happened to me.

"I love you, baby," I told her.

Corliss' fingers caressed my cheek. "I love you, Swede." I slowed for the lights in Corona Del Mar. "You'll be good to me?" Corliss asked.

"As good as I know how," I promised. "But let's get one thing straight. I'm not going to live on the money the Purple Parrot brings in. Maybe I won't buy a farm.

Maybe I won't have enough left. If not, I'll get a job shoreside until I do. What I'm getting at is, *I* support the family."

Her hand dropped back to my thigh again. "You *are* sweet, Swede."

I wished she'd stop squeezing my thigh. At least until I could do something about it. As we neared Laguna Beach I asked her if she was hungry.

"Not very," Corliss said. "Let's wait until we get to San Diego to eat."

It was dark now. I was driving with the brights on. As we rounded a bend in the road the headlights picked up the Beachcomber Bar.

It was a big, unpainted barn plastered with soft-drink signs. Behind it the ocean was in motion again, rolling, surging, flecked with white caps. I thought of the rocks at the foot of the cliff and shuddered. The rocks and the waves had done plenty to Wolkowysk by now. I was foolish to worry about fingerprints. When the ocean got through with the Buick, there wouldn't even be any wheel.

Corliss deliberately looked away as we passed the bar.

I began to sweat again. Wolkowysk had been missed by now. If he owned the bar, his employees were beginning to ask questions. If he had been an employee, his employer was beginning to wonder where he was.

I asked Corliss if Wolkowysk had been married.

She almost screamed the words, repressed hysteria bubbling in her. "Can't we forget about Wolkowysk?"

I said, "I wish we could."

We ate in San Diego at the best hotel, then drove south through the night, under the stars, with the windows up and the heater on and the smell of her filling the car. On my way to be married or not, I drove with only one thing on my mind, acutely conscious of Corliss, memory incubating the butterflies in my stomach. Maybe the respect and trust and other things would come later. Right now I wanted *her*.

We had no trouble at the barrier. We were one of a hundred cars, possibly two hundred, filled with tourists, cheaters, gamblers. Down for the evening or a long weekend. Come to Mexico to buy a pair of huaraches for Aunt Bessie in Sioux Falls, to gamble, to grow horns on some trusting husband or wife who thought they were at a P.T.A. convention or a meeting of the Loyal Order of Moose.

The Mexican license bureau was closed. I'd expected that. There was a bar on the main drag with a faded sign that proclaimed it to be the longest bar in the world. I parked Corliss at a table and bought her a rum Collins to work on. Then I brushed off my rusty Spanish and buttonholed the first cop I met on the street.

"Puede recomendarme un abogado... que... comprende inglés?" I asked him.

The policeman nodded. "Yeah. Sure thing, mate." He pointed across the street to a lighted second-floor window. "Right over there. José Sánchez Avarillo. José is a graduate of Stanford and he speaks perfect English. Tell him that Nick sent you."

I walked across the street and up a flight of stairs. Avarillo was young, good-looking, smooth. He looked like the kind of lawyer I wanted, one who knew all the local angles.

We gave each other the *"Buenas noches, señor"* routine. Then I counted ten ten-dollar bills on his desk. "For you, *señor."*

Avarillo eyed the bills. *"Si, señor.* What can I do for you?"

I said, "I want a marriage license."

"Si?"

"For one Mrs. John Mason, a widow, and Swen Nelson, single," I picked one of the pencils from his desk and wrote the names on a pad. "Plus a priest or a judge or a justice of the peace. It doesn't matter, as long as whoever you get is legally empowered to marry us."

Avarillo studied the names. "This must be done tonight, *señor?"*

I gave it back to him in Spanish. *"Hoy."*

He counted the bills and put them in his vest pocket. "It shall be as you wish, *Señor* Nelson." He leaned back in his swivel chair. "But, as you must realize, it is long after hours for such matters. I shall be obliged to contact the license clerk at his *casa.* Also the custodian of the courthouse. Then there is the judge." His smile was bland. "So, while you have paid me my fee," he rubbed his thumb and forefinger together, "there will be other minor expenses. Shall we say another hundred dollars?"

This after he had my money in his pocket. I named him. "You sonofabitch."

Avarillo continued to smile. "Be that as it may. Would you disappoint the lovely *señora, señor?* And I am certain she is lovely."

There was nothing I could do but go along. He knew it. I counted another hundred dollars on his desk.

Avarillo put it with the other bills. *"Muchisimas gracias, señor.* If you and Mrs. Mason will return to this office in half an hour, both the license you request and a qualified judge will be waiting."

I walked back to the longest bar in the world. A dark-complected little drunk with a long, scraggly mustache was bothering Corliss. He'd plopped himself down in the chair across from her and was smiling in what he hoped was an ingratiating manner, meanwhile spitting a stream of words in some language with which I wasn't familiar. As I came up behind him he reached across the table for her hand and tried to stroke it.

Corliss looked terrified.

I yanked the little drunk to his feet by his coat collar. He was stronger than he looked; squat, broad-shouldered, with the bulging muscles of a man who worked hard with his hands. He twisted out of my grip and, standing spraddle-legged beside the table, turned his stream of words in my direction. He sounded like middle or southern Europe to me.

"You got any idea what he's talking about?" I asked Corliss.

She got to her feet white-faced. "No. Get me out of here, Swede. He frightens me."

I started to walk her down the aisle between the tables and the bar. The little guy blocked our path. I couldn't tell if he was mad or trying to be friendly. Then he reached out a work-gnarled hand and patted Corliss' backside.

"N-i-i-ce."

Corliss screamed as he touched her. I slapped him so hard he went to the floor.

The Mexican waiter came up to our table. "What's the matter here?"

I said, "He insulted the *señora*."

The waiter was philosophic. "The man is dronk, *señor*." He helped the man in the blue serge suit to his feet and propped him against the bar so he could get drunker.

I dropped a bill on the table and walked Corliss to the door. Sagging against the bar, blood trickling down his chin, the drunk continued to curse us through his mustache.

I walked Corliss the length of the business district and back on the other side of the street before she recovered her composure. By then it was time to go back to Avarillo's office.

I tried to keep my voice casual. "It's a long drive back to the Parrot. After we're married, why not stay here tonight?"

Corliss was still upset by the scene in the bar, but she managed a smile for me. "Whatever you say, Swede."

I called a hotel and reserved a room. Then I bought a bottle of rum and walked upstairs to be married.

It wasn't much of a wedding. The judge was a dried-up little Mexican in a dirty white linen suit. He mumbled through nine-o'clock shadow with Avarillo interpreting for Corliss' sake. The ceremony seemed short to mean so much. The pride of the bench was drunk and eager to get back to whatever Avarillo's phone call had interrupted. But his words were just as binding as if we were being married by a priest in St. Patrick's Cathedral.

When we finished we all had a drink, the witnesses

too, a doe-eyed tart and a pock-marked cab driver, Avarillo graciously furnishing the glasses.

Then the tart and the cab driver signed the wedding certificate and left, supporting the judge between them. Avarillo folded the certificate and the properly filled-in license and handed them to Corliss.

"May God bless your marriage, *señora*."

"Thank you," she said soberly.

He corked the still half-filled bottle of rum and put it in his filing cabinet. For a souvenir, no doubt. Then he shook hands with me.

"May you both be very happy, *señor*."

He looked very pleased with Avarillo. He had reason to be. Avarillo had just made Avarillo the best part of two hundred dollars.

Corliss and I walked back down the sagging stairs, the wooden risers squeaking under our feet like happy mice, my left arm around her waist.

Tijuana's main drag was swarming with tourists and teen-aged sailors from the naval base at Dago. Most of the kids were a little high, their money burning holes in the pockets they wished they had, buying junk in the cheap stores, having their pictures taken on burros. Mixed in with the crowd were a few uniformed cops and a scattering of Mexican streetwalkers. With something else to sell. The cops kept their eyes on the streetwalkers. The street-walkers kept their eyes on the sailors. The sailors kept their eyes on the streetwalkers. Everybody happy. Juke boxes and dance orchestras blared in every other doorway. No one paid any attention to us. No one gave a damn that we were married except Mr. and Mrs. Swen Nelson.

I walked Corliss for two blocks, just getting used to being married. I liked it. It was like walking on tiptoe over a cloud, a big white fleecy cloud stuffed with foam-rubber mattresses.

There was a bar at the far end of the block. I bought another bottle. Then we took a cab to the hotel.

The room was nice, big, old-fashioned, with a high ceiling and tall windows. It reminded me of the rooms in the old part of the Hotel Grande Ancira in Monterrey. Both hotels had been built when labor and materials were cheap. The tub in the bathroom was marble and almost big enough to swim in.

When the bellboy had left with my buck I opened the bottle of rum and half filled two water glasses.

"Happy, honey?" I asked Corliss.

"Very happy," she said.

Both her smile and her voice were vague.

I took off my coat and loosened my tie. "What's the matter? Something wrong?"

"No. Nothing at all," Corliss assured me. She sat on the edge of the bed. She kicked off her shoes. She wriggled her toes for a moment in almost sensuous enjoyment. Then she unfastened and took off her stockings.

I took off my shirt and loosened my belt. "I'll bet the folks back at the court will be surprised when we tell them we're married."

"I imagine they will," Corliss said.

She stood up and pulled her dress over her head. Then she unhooked her bra, uncupping her breasts one at a time.

It was like watching a lovely strip tease.

I unlaced my shoes, looking up at her.

Corliss wriggled her lush white hips out of her black lace panties, then sat back on the bed and lifted her honey-colored hair away from the back of her neck. "How long do you think it will take the police to find out that Jerry is missing?"

I said, "This is a hell of a time to bring that up."

Corliss sipped at the rum in the glass she'd set on the chair by the bed. "I'm sorry."

I finished undressing and lighted a cigarette with shaking fingers. "I hope they never find him."

"So do I," Corliss said.

She lay back on the bed, one leg straight, one tanned knee raised and moving slowly from side to side. There was no passion in her eyes as she looked at me. There was only a mild, almost disinterested, speculation. Her smile seemed forced and false.

I felt suddenly sick. I didn't know what I'd expected of marriage, but this wasn't it.

Corliss' smile grew even more false. "What's the matter, honey? Why are you looking at me like that?"

I sat on the bed beside her. The mirror in the dresser was tilted so I could see our bodies. Even Corliss' body seemed changed. It looked, somehow, used and worn. She said she loved me. She couldn't wait three days to be married. This was our wedding night. But instead of being eager with desire, she was lying dully, passively, patiently.

"What's the matter, honey?" she repeated.

"Nothing at all," I lied.

She pulled me down to her. "Then love me, honey. Please."

She was my wife. I'd killed a man for her. I wanted her. I took her. For a moment I hoped I was wrong. But I wasn't. We were just two people in bed.

I glanced sideways in the mirror at the moving reflection. Corliss' moans and pretended passion were as false as her sighs had been. All the new Mrs. Nelson was doing was going through the motions.

She might have been chewing gum or paying a grocery bill.

The magic of the madness on the cliff was gone. All there was between us was flesh.

Chapter Eleven

It had been night, then morning, now it was evening again. So what? I was having a hell of a time, even for a sailor, spending my honeymoon with a bottle in Cottage Number 3 of the Purple Parrot Tourist Court and Bar on U.S. Highway 101, just north of San Diego.

I lay rolling rum in my mouth, liking the taste of it, listening to the breakers kiss the beach, hearing the swish of fast moving traffic, the cheerful chirping of the crickets, smelling night-flowering nicotiana and gardenias.

For a guy who had started out with good intentions, I sure was still a hell of a long way from Hibbing, Minnesota.

I was back at the Purple Parrot. I knew that. I remembered Corliss crying when we'd checked out of the hotel in Tijuana. I remembered the hot Mexican morning sun. I remembered bouncing a Mexican cop off a brick wall when he had intimated I was too drunk to drive.

Still more of the night and day just past came back. I remembered Corliss giving the cop money, a lot of money, my money. To smear on his pride, no doubt. I remembered Corliss promising the cop she'd drive, vaguely, as in a dream. I remembered her face white and set, her long honey-colored hair streaming out behind her in the wind as she drove with the top down. To sober up her bridegroom.

I remembered her asking me, "For God's sake, what's wrong with you, Swede? Why did you have to get drunk last night, of all times?"

I threw the empty bottle at the wall. To hear it smash. Then I rolled off the bed onto the deck and crawled into the head on my hands and knees, barely making seaway. I was too drunk to stand under the shower. I filled the tub with cold water and lay in it, letting the water run, rubbing the cold into my scalp and flesh. I wanted desperately to get sober. So I could walk up to the bar and tie on a real one this time.

I lay in the water a long time. I was debating getting out when the spring on the screen door screeched. The door banged shut again. High heels clicked across asphalt tile. Whoever it was was in a hurry.

"Mr. Nelson." The voice was urgent, feminine, familiar.

I got out of the tub and wrapped a towel around me and walked out in the living room. It was Mamie, with a steaming mug of coffee in one hand. I fastened the towel more securely. "What's the big idea?"

She looked at me the way she had the first morning. As if she liked what she saw. Then her lips twisted as if she were going to cry. She didn't. Instead she offered me the mug.

"Drink this, Mr. Nelson. Please."

The black coffee tasted good. I drained the mug and set it on the dresser. Next to what was left of my money. "Thanks. You're a good girl, Mamie. But I asked you a question."

"What?"

I wiped my lips on the back of my hand. "What's the big idea?"

Mamie looked over her shoulder at the night outside the screen door, then back at me. Her firm young breasts rose and fell with her rapid breathing. She was either frightened or she had hurried.

She looked back at me. "You won't laugh at me?"

"I won't laugh at you."

"You're in danger here, Mr. Nelson. Please believe me. Please get dressed. And leave."

It was the third time she'd pulled the same gag. I picked my shorts from a chair and slid them on, under the towel. "What sort of danger?"

She played the same old record. "I don't know."

"Who says I should leave?"

"I do."

"Just you?"

"Just me."

I put on my pants and combed my hair. I still felt naked without my cap. I put it on.

Mamie's lips twisted in a wry smile. "That's right. Cock it over one eye. Look tough. Act tough. When you're a pushover inside. Show them that no one or nothing can hurt you. That you don't give a damn for God or the Devil."

I grinned at her. "What's the matter, kid? Jealous of Corliss?"

Mamie thought that one over. "No. I don't think it's that."

I tucked my shirt into my pants and knotted my tie. "Now can I ask you a question?"

There was a breathless quality to her voice. "I don't see why not."

"How come a pretty girl like you married a fellow like Meek? If I'm not being too personal, it seems to me that you could have done better."

Her smile turned even wrier. "That's because you weren't born in a small South Dakota town that had three girls to every boy."

"You were?"

"I was. In a family of four girls."

"All of them as pretty as you?"

The compliment pleased her. "You do think I'm pretty?"

I took my uniform coat from its hanger. "I think you're very pretty. I think you're one of the prettiest girls I've ever met." I meant it.

Mamie was still naïve enough to blush. "Thank you, Mr. Nelson."

I was generous. "Call me Swede."

"Swede, then."

I slipped into my coat and buttoned it. "But you still haven't told me why you married Meek."

She said, "To get out of Murdock, South Dakota. To get a few pretty clothes. To see some new faces. To go somewhere besides a movie on Saturday night and church on Sunday and Wednesday. You were born in a small town, too. But you're a man. You've been all over the world. You've done interesting things all your life. You don't know what it means to be so bored that you jump at the chance to marry the first carnival barker who asks you. Just to get out of a town you hate."

That explained Meek. He looked like a carny. But

what he was doing working as a gardener was beyond me.

"You love the guy?"

"We're married."

I gave her a bit of advice. "If you want to stay married, you'd better get out of here. He threatened to stick a knife in me if he even caught us together."

Mamie lifted her head. "He wouldn't dare. He's afraid of you. I heard him tell Wally so. He said, 'I'm leery of that guy Nelson.'"

I didn't get the play. I gripped Mamie by the shoulders. "Look. So something funny is going on. So I'm in danger here. Why should you give a damn?"

Mamie looked me in the eyes. "I know it sounds funny. I'm nothing to you. I'm just a girl who manages a tourist court that your wife owns. But maybe you're something to me. Maybe you're part of a dream I dreamed a long time ago. Back in Murdock. Maybe you're the kind of man I used to dream I'd meet."

"You've told me that before."

"Before I knew you were going to marry Corliss. And it is just as true now."

This going around the pin was making my head ache. I didn't want to think. I wanted to stop thinking. I wanted a slug of rum. I wanted a lot of slugs. I tilted her chin. "What do you know about Corliss?"

"Nothing. I never saw her before we came here to work."

"Then what's this danger business?"

Mamie met my eyes. "I don't know. I just know you are in danger. There's something awfully wrong about this court."

"In what way?"

"I can't explain. It—it's just a feeling."

"In other words, womanly intuition."

"I suppose you could call it that."

I straightened the set of my coat. "Well, thanks a lot for the coffee. Now, if you'll excuse me, I have a date. With a bottle."

Mamie barred the way to the door with her body. "No. You've got to listen to me, Swede. She's hurt you already, hasn't she? Somehow she's made you bitter."

"Who?"

"Corliss."

I gripped Mamie's wrists and tried to pull her hands away from my lapels. "Let's leave Corliss out of this."

Mamie got hysterical. "This is still a free country. I'll say what I please. About anyone."

I tightened my fingers on her wrists. Mamie screamed. Not loud. In her throat.

"You're hurting me, Swede."

I looked at her wrists. There was a nasty burn on one of them. "How did you get that?" I asked her.

Mamie said, "On the iron."

"What iron?"

She began to cry softly. "The one I used the first day you came here. To press your uniform and iron your shirt."

I pushed her away from me. The edge of the bed struck the back of her knees. Mamie sprawled on the bed on her back, her circular skirt flying up as she fell.

"Now I know you're lying," I said. "You're just trying to make trouble between us. That's what you are. A troublemaker. Corliss washed and ironed my shirt and pressed my uniform."

Mamie raised herself on one elbow. "Corliss told you that?"

"She did."

"In bed with you last night in Tijuana, I suppose?"

I shook my head. "No. In her car the night before. After she got me out of jail."

Mamie's eyes turned sullen. Her lower lip thrust out. She reminded me of Corliss. "You don't believe a word I've said, do you?"

"You haven't said anything."

"I told you there was something wrong about this court."

"Sure. There's something wrong about all tourist courts. They charge too much."

Mamie wet her lips with her tongue. The sullen look left her face. Color began to creep into her cheeks. "You think I'm pretty, don't you, Swede?"

"I've told you so several times."

"Have I a pretty body?"

I looked at her exposed thighs. "You have a very pretty body."

The color in Mamie's cheeks deepened. "Will you believe I really think you're in danger and get out of here if I do something I've never done before?"

"What?" I asked flatly.

"Cheat on my husband," Mamie said.

I lighted a cigarette. "When?"

She licked her lips again. "Right now."

I laughed at her. "You'd be afraid to. Meek would kill you."

"I wouldn't care."

"You're kidding."

Mamie began to have trouble with her breathing. "If you think so, close that door."

I closed the door. To see how far she'd go. When I turned back to the bed she'd already slipped her dress over her head and was trying to unhook her bra. Mamie meant what she said. She was willing to sail the full distance.

I walked back to the bed and sat beside her. By the time I sat down she had her bra off. She was as lovely as Corliss. Possibly even more so. There was a fresh, almost virginal quality to her body. Just looking at her excited me. It made me a little sick to think of her being married to a man like Meek. There was no telling how he abused her.

I put my hand over hers. "Uh-uh honey," I said. "I'm married to Corliss. You're married to Meek. Remember?"

Her breath was sweet and hot on my cheek. "What difference does our being married make?"

I admitted, "In most cases it wouldn't mean a thing. In this instance, quite a bit. If you and I had just been married, you wouldn't want me to sleep with Corliss, would you?"

Mamie snuggled her cheek against my chest and began to cry. I tranferred my hand to her back and held her the way I might have held my kid sister, if I'd had one.

"Look," I said. "Don't get me wrong. God knows I'm not one of His angels. I'd love to. I know it would be very wonderful."

She sniffed, "You—you wanted me the other morning. You told me to either come and get in your bed or get out."

I stroked her back. "That was the other morning. Now it wouldn't be right for either of us. And no matter how wonderful it was, neither of us would be very proud of ourselves, would we?"

Mamie snuggled her cheek even closer to my chest. "You are nice, Swede. You're good. And fine. And decent. That hard-boiled act of yours is all an act. You're just as nice as I knew you would be."

I tilted Mamie's chin and kissed her wet lips. "O.K. So I'm in danger. I believe you. Can you be more definite?"

She shook her head. "No. I can't."

I thought a moment, then risked the question. "What do you know about Jerry Wolkowysk?"

Mamie wiped her eyes with a lock of hair. "He's a bartender at the Beachcomber who tried to make headway with Corliss, and couldn't. Then to get even he told it all up and down the beach that she was bad, that she would do it with anyone for twenty dollars."

"Would she?"

Mamie was fair. She shook her head. "No. In the two years I've been here I've never known Corliss to allow *any* man in her cottage. Except Wally on Wednesday nights. And now you."

"Wolkowysk never came here?"

Mamie bobbed her head. "Quite frequently. He was

here just the night before last. That is, in the bar. He was drunk, nasty drunk. And when I tried to close the bar at two, he cursed me. Something awful. In Polish, or whatever he is. So I had to keep the bar open until ten minutes after two."

"What happened then?"

"Wally came back from checking the books with Corliss and put him out. Why?"

I rested my head against hers a moment. Then I asked if she would do me a favor.

Mamie said, "Of course."

"Forget that I mentioned his name."

Then I got out of the cabin fast. Before I reverted to normal and stopped being so goddamn noble.

Chapter Twelve

I walked the long way around the court to the bar. The "No Vacancy" sign was flying. There was a car in every port. Cars from Kansas, Nebraska, Maine, Missouri, Texas, Wyoming, Illinois, Rhode Island.

Meek was setting out pansy plants around the bole of one of the spotlighted palms. The guy got to his feet as I neared him, his job more important than his wife.

His voice was a rat-tailed file rasping across my nerves. "Good evening, Mr. Nelson." He was making an obvious effort to be nice, but his lined face looked somehow sinister in the spotlight. "May I offer my congratulations on your marriage to Mrs. Mason? I hope you both are very happy."

I said, "Thank you," and walked on, ignoring his hand.

I liked the guy better when he'd been nasty, threatening to stick a knife in me if I didn't let Mamie alone. I hoped she'd be gone by the time I got back to my cottage. I liked the kid. But that was all that it ever could be. I had a wife now. I loved her. I'd dropped my hook. I was anchored.

The bar and restaurant were doing a good business. There was a line of out-of-state cars parked under the neon parrot. I smoked a cigarette under a palm, listening to the pound of the waves. I almost wished I were in Hibbing, somewhere in the Sulu Sea, anywhere but where I was, having to go in and face Corliss.

So why *had* I got drunk? All right, I was willing to bite. Why had I?

Corliss had been sweet. She hadn't denied me a thing. She loved me. She wanted to marry me. We had been married. She had been very happy about it. She had repeated her "I do's," with all the fervor of a drowning woman snatching at a life preserver.

It could be I was wrong. It could be she was fine and good. It could be I had been so keyed up in Tijuana that I had mistaken a desire to please me for professional practice. It could be that sex didn't mean as much to her as it did to me, that she had to be abnormally excited emotionally before she reacted physically. That would explain her passion on the cliff the night we had dumped Wolkowysk. It could be she had an emotional block of some kind. I wiped the leather sweat band of my cap.

God almighty. What if I had to kill a man every time I wanted to really arouse her?

I flicked my butt into the night. Sparks skittered along the highway. Then I walked into the bar and sat on a chrome-and-leather stool between two tourists.

Wally set a bottle of rum in front of me. "Congratulations, Mr. Nelson. Miss Mason—that is, I should say, Mrs. Nelson—tells me you were married last night in Tijuana."

I half filled the old-fashioned glass he'd put on the wood. "That's right."

Wally didn't offer to shake hands. He didn't hope we'd be happy. I drank my drink and poured another, wondering where Corliss was, afraid to ask.

The tourist on my right finished his chicken-in-a-basket and walked out. I lowered the bottle another inch. It was a funny feeling. I felt as if I were running, sitting still. Wally, Corliss, Wolkowysk, the Purple Parrot were shadowy figments in a dream. Only the rum was real.

I started to pour another drink and the heavy-set waitress who'd served my breakfast the morning before set a sizzling steak in front of me.

"Doctor's orders, Mr. Nelson."

I asked, "What's your name?"

She smiled. "Cora."

"Where's Corliss, Cora?" I asked her.

"Mrs. Nelson's in the kitchen," she said.

She picked the chicken basket and a butt-littered coffee cup from the wood. I picked at the steak. A few moments later Sheriff Cooper came in, alone, and walked up to where I was sitting.

I scowled at him over another filled glass. "Now what?"

Cooper sat on the vacated stool, "Don't be so touchy, Nelson. No one's trying to push you around. A complaint was made. A warrant was sworn out. I had to make an arrest."

I ate a few bites of the steak.

The white-haired sheriff lighted a cigar. "In fact, I just dropped in to tell you that I've located one of the avocado ranchers you mentioned as witnesses to your fight with Tony Corado. A fellow by the name of Hayes."

My drinking was compulsory. I didn't want another drink. I poured one. "So?"

"So Hayes says that even if Tony should die, it was

106

self-defense on your part. He said Corado came at you with a sap and all you did was defend yourself."

"I told you and Farrell that the night you arrested me and made me make bond."

"So you did," Cooper agreed.

I sipped at the rum I had poured. Then, hoping my voice sounded casual, I asked, "What does the barman say? What was his name—Jerry?"

Cooper puffed at his cigar. "I haven't been able to locate Wolkowysk yet. He hasn't shown up for work for two days."

I finished the rum in the glass. It failed to melt the lump of ice in my stomach. "Funny," I said. "Funny."

Cooper didn't seem perturbed about it. "He's probably on a binge. The lad who owns the Beachcomber says that Wolkowysk is a periodic drinker."

It was a break I hadn't expected. It could be a few days, possibly even a week or two, before Wolkowysk would be thought of as "missing."

Wally leaned on the bar. "What you drinking, Sheriff? On the house."

"You know better than that," Cooper said.

Wally grinned at him. "This is a special occasion."

"What's special about it?"

Wally inclined his fat head at me. "Nelson and Miss Mason were married last night." He managed to make it sound dirty. "In Tijuana."

Cooper let Wally draw him a short beer. I poured another double. Automatically.

Cooper lifted his glass. "Good luck, Nelson. I hope you both will be very happy."

For some reason it struck me funny. I hope you'll be very happy. From Avarillo. From Meek. And now from Sheriff Cooper. Like so many empty-headed purple parrots. What the hell? A guy didn't get married with the intention of being *un*happy.

I gripped my glass so hard it cracked, cutting my palm in a couple of places. I laid the broken glass on the bar and wrapped a napkin around my hand. "Another glass, please."

Wally gave me another glass. "Hadn't you better go easy, fellow? You're drunk as hell right now."

I felt nasty. I talked the same way. "You telling me how to run my life?"

"Far be it from me," Wally said. He moved off down the bar to serve a customer.

I poured rum in the fresh glass. I knew what would happen if I drank it with only three bites of steak in my stomach. I drank it.

Sheriff Cooper pushed his white Stetson back on his head. "You're a pretty heavy drinker, aren't you, son?"

"When I'm ashore."

"How long are you staying ashore?"

"From now on." I meant it to sound funny. "Why should I work? I own half of a prosperous tourist court now."

It came out flat. With nothing funny about it. Cooper said, "Oh, I see." His tone was disapproving.

The rum was taking a good bite now, magnifying the clatter of dishes and the voices in the bar. The stool was beginning to revolve. I started to set him straight. In no uncertain language. But before I could, Corliss came out of the kitchen. She looked cool and fresh and sweet in a white nylon uniform like Cora's, with a big purple parrot embroidered on her left shoulder.

Standing beside the stool, she squeezed my arm. "Hello, honey. The steak all right?"

I said the steak was fine. "What you doing in the kitchen?"

Corliss said, "One of the girls quit without notice. So I'm giving the cook a hand."

Cooper took off his hat. "I hear you and Nelson were married last night. Congratulations."

"Thank you, Sheriff," Corliss said.

There was a slightly breathless quality to her voice. The white uniform hugging her body made her look innocent and untouched.

Sheriff Cooper hoped Corliss would be happy. He hoped we both would be happy, and left.

Corliss sat on the stool beside me.

I said, "I'm sorry about last night."

Corliss played with one of my fingers. "Forget it, Swede. You were just emotionally overwrought." Her eyes were worried. "But you've got to stop this drinking. We've too much at stake. What did Sheriff Cooper want?"

I tried to tell her, my tongue thick in my mouth. "He said he jush—" I backed off and tried it again, slowly. "He said—"

The rum hit me then. In the back of the head. Like the smash of a winch handle. My tongue filled my mouth. The bar tilted at a crazy angle. I was afraid the rum bottle was going to slide off and spill on Corliss' uniform. To keep that from happening, I made a wild grab for the bottle and the stool went around and around and I wound up flat on my back on the floor with the blue-nosed tourists in the booths *tch-tching* and Corliss sobbing:

"Oh, Swede. Oh, my darling!"

I was lying in a mixture of broken glass and rum. I tried to get up and couldn't. Wally came around the bar, apologetic. "I should have refused to serve him." He got an arm around my shoulders and lifted me to a sitting position. "Geez. He drank a pint in ten minutes. On an empty stomach."

Corliss continued to cry.

Then Meek crawled out from somewhere, out of the baseboard, possibly, and he and Wally and Corliss walked me out of the bar.

Sheriff Cooper was kicking one of his tires thoughtfully. As we passed him, Cooper said, "I was afraid that was going to happen."

"Where do you want him, Mrs. Nelson?" Wally asked.

Corliss sobbed, "In my cottage."

She opened the screen door. Wally and Meek carried me inside and dumped me on her bed.

Meek gave his opinion as he unlaced my shoes. My shoes thudded to the floor. "You know something, Mrs. Nelson? Mr. Nelson acts to me like a guy with something on his mind."

Corliss said fiercely, "Get out of here. Both of you."

"Whatever you say, Mrs. Nelson," Wally said.

The spring on the screen door screeched, then twanged. I could hear water running in the bathroom.

Then Corliss sat down on the edge of the bed and wiped my face with a towel that had been soaked in cold water. She unloosened my tie. She unfastened the top button of my shirt, her fingers trembling.

"I love you, Corliss," I told her.

Corliss cried even harder. "Then why are you doing this to me?"

I tried to explain. I couldn't. All that came out of my mouth was words, while the hurt stayed locked inside me. How explain hunger, a hunger for something you've never known?

You're born in a small inland town. Both your parents die when you're a kid. You run away and go to sea when you're fifteen. You're big for your age. You lie. When you're twenty you're six feet two with hands like picnic hams. You weigh two hundred pounds, every ounce of it muscle and leather. You're blond, with light blue eyes. Eyes that go back to some big Swede in armor.

Women like you. And all the women you meet are the same. In Lisbon, Suez, Capetown. In Mozambique, Kimberly, Leopoldville. In Colón, Rio, Lima. In Boston, San Pedro, Seattle.

"Hello, sailor. Lonely?"

Three little words. A password and a passport. Drop your anchor and climb aboard. You're always welcome, sailor. As long as you have money. An escudo, eight shillings, ten pesos, a few francs, a handful of kopeks, a Hershey bar, a package of cigarettes, five dollars.

And sometimes it's for free. A few laughs. A few drinks. A good line. With married dames, cheating on some guy who loves them.

But all the time you know there's another facet to sex. You stand watch with your thoughts on a bridge. Under the stars. Night after night. For years. On oceans all over the world. Just you and God and the helmsman awake. In the middle of a phosphorescent sea stretching out to all hell and Judgment Day.

Somewhere there is one woman. A woman who's fine and clean and good. The woman who is going to be the mother of your children. And her love is going to wash the slate. Her love is going to make you as clean as she is. Maybe you'll live on a farm. Maybe you'll live in town. Maybe you'll run a highway tourist court. It doesn't matter. Nothing matters but that you're together.

You meet her. The woman. The dream. Under adverse circumstances. But you know her the moment you see her. You've come into port at long last. The sailor is home from the sea. You marry the dream. It's yours now, for keeps.

Then there's a certain look in her eyes, a certain false enthusiasm when she comes into your arms, a certain professional adeptness. And you begin to wonder.

Which is it? Your own goddamn dirty mind? Or her?

Corliss sobbed, "Have I done or said anything to hurt your feelings, darling?"

It was difficult for me to breathe. The rum had undermined the front legs of the bed, making it tilt at an angle. "No," I said. "Of course not."

Corliss lay down on the bed and pressed her body close to mine. "Is it because of Jerry? Because of what he did to me?"

"No."

She whispered in my ear. "Because of what we had

to do to him?"

"No."

My left hand was resting on her hip. Corliss played with my fingers a moment. "Don't you like the way I make love? Don't you like to love me?"

I raised myself on one elbow. I said, "For God's sake, Corliss. Please."

Corliss kept on playing with my fingers. "I asked you a question."

I pressed my face against hers. "Yeah. Sure. You know I'm crazy about you."

"Prove it," Corliss said. "Prove it." Her mouth hovered over mine. "Prove you love me, Swede. Or are you too drunk?"

"I never get *that* drunk," I said.

The walls of the cottage faded out. We were back on the cliff again, all the mad magic of the night intact, Corliss no longer pretending, every bit as passionate as she'd been the first time.

She had reason. I'd just killed another man for her. The man I'd hoped to be when I'd told Ginty good-by and bought a ticket for Hibbing, Minnesota. I loved her. I'd never loved any woman as much as I loved Corliss. I would always love her. It was Corliss and Swede from now on.

But no one needed to tell me. I knew. So she drove a green Cadillac. So she owned a two-hundred-thousand-dollar tourist court named the Purple Parrot on U.S. Highway 101, just north of San Diego. It wouldn't change a thing if she owned the highway.

My love was a high-class tramp.

Chapter Thirteen

It was two o'clock the next afternoon when Sheriff Cooper dropped in again. He had Harris and a third man with him, the third man a stranger to me.

"Hi, mate," Cooper said.

I touched the visor of my cap. "Hi. Don't tell me Corado had a relapse."

"No. I'm not here on his account," Cooper said.

Wally turned the radio on the back bar to a whisper. The sudden silence hurt my ears.

Cooper pushed his white Stetson back on his head. Then he took it off and wiped the leather sweatband with his handkerchief. "No," he repeated finally. "As I told you last night, the chances are you won't even have to stand trial on that score. Or were you too drunk to remember that, Nelson?"

I said, "I remember it distinctly. That's why I was a little surprised to see you again so soon."

The five of us were alone in the bar. Harris sat on a bar stool facing me. "Yeah. Corado is doing fine. We're more interested in Wolkowysk."

I played it dumb. "Wolkowysk?"

"You don't remember him?"

I looked at Sheriff Cooper. "Oh. You mean Jerry, the barman up at the Beachcomber. He came back to work, huh? He confirmed what the rancher told you."

Cooper returned his hat to his head. "No."

I asked, "No what? He didn't come back to work or didn't confirm it?"

"Neither," Harris said. "He's dead."

I timed it to say it with Wally. "Dead?"

Cooper nodded. "At least, that's the assumption. He's been missing for two days. And this morning two surf fishermen found what was left of his car at the foot of a cliff about ten miles up the road from here."

I said, "I'm a son-of-a-gun."

Wally shook his head. "I had an idea something like that might happen."

The man with Cooper and Harris leaned one elbow on the wood. "What do you mean by that, bartender?"

Wally explained. "On account of the condition he was in when he was in here the other night. I'd been checking the books with Miss Mason—Mrs. Nelson now—see? And when I came back to the bar around two-ten, maybe two-fifteen, Mrs. Meek is hopping mad, bawling even, because Wolkowysk is in here stinking drunk and won't let her close up the bar."

"What's your name, bartender?" the man asked.

"Wally. Wally Connors. Why?"

"Let's just say I'm interested. You got a record, Connors? You on the book anywhere?"

Wally was indignant. "Not me, mister. And I'm in good standing with the union." He insisted on showing the man his paid-up card.

The man didn't seem much interested. "Let's get back to Wolkowysk. What made you think something might happen to him?"

"I told you," Wally said. "Because he was so drunk. I said to myself, If that guy is driving—oh, brother."

"I thought that according to California law you aren't supposed to sell to intoxicated men."

"We don't. As soon as I see the condition he's in, I raise hell with Mrs. Meek. But she said she only sold him three drinks and she thought he must have taken goof balls with them."

"That checks," the man told Cooper. "How was Wolkowysk acting when you came in, Connors?"

Wally spread his fat palms on the bar. "Confidentially, between us, not like a gentleman should."

"What do you mean by that?"

Wally confided, "He was making not proper suggestions to Mrs. Meek. Offering her money to go out in his car with him."

I began to get a better picture of what had happened. Wolkowysk had built up his yen on Mamie, then taken it out on Corliss. I was glad I'd killed the bastard.

Wally continued indignantly. "I tell him nice, see, it's after two o'clock and will he please leave so I can close the bar. And he stops picking on Mrs. Meek and begins to cuss me." Wally grew even more indignant. "Not only in English. In Polish or Russian, even."

"Then what happened?"

Wally straightened to his full six feet of blubber. "I stand his talk as long as I can. Patient, a gentleman, see? The customer is always right. Then I get a bellyful and I grab him by his collar and his trousers and I throw him out on his ass. Why? Did I do wrong?"

The soft-spoken man laughed. "No. That was about all you could do. What time was this, Connors?"

"Like I say, after two. Maybe two-fifteen."

"You saw him get in his car?"

"No. I don't pay any attention. I locked the front door, told Mrs. Meek good night, and went to bed."

"How about you, Nelson?" Harris asked. "Did you see Wolkowysk Wednesday night?"

I looked at Harris over a fresh-poured glass of rum. "Why should I have seen him?"

"They're saying along the highway that Wolkowysk was sweet on your girl."

"My wife."

"Your wife, then."

A drop of sweat zigzagged down my spine. I wondered where I'd slipped up. *If* I had. "Why, yes. Come to think of it," I admitted. "I did see him. Earlier in the evening. After I got back from posting bail in that Corado affair. He was at the end of the bar with three other men."

Sheriff Cooper said, "You didn't tell me that last night."

I grinned at him. "I was drunk. Remember?"

"You spoke to Wolkowysk?"

I told him the truth. "No. I wasn't even sure it was him. He looked like I remembered the bartender at the Beachcomber looked, but I'd been pretty high there, too. Even if I had been certain it was him, I doubt if I'd have spoken."

"Why not?"

"Because if I had talked to him and the Corado affair

does come to trial, some vote-hunting D.A. would probably have accused me of bribing him to color his testimony in my favor."

"Where do you come in on this sailor?" the soft spoken man asked me.

I sipped at the rum in my glass. "That's a long story."

He leaned against the bar. "Go ahead. Tell it, mate. I've got all the time in the world."

My head ached. My collar was too tight. He was law of some kind, important law. It was in his voice, his bearing. His eyes were shrewd, evaluating. He smelled like a fed to me.

"You have a right to question me?"

He said, "I have." It was a flat statement.

I wiped my mouth with the back of my hand. Then I gave him as much as I thought was safe, as much as he could find out elsewhere.

I told him how I had been paid off after three years in the islands, how I'd intended to head out Minnesota way but had gone on a drunk instead and wound up at the Beachcomber, where I had got into a crap game and a brawl with a Mexican Fancy Dan.

"You damn near killed him," Harris said. "Those fists of yours are lethal weapons, Nelson."

I ignored Harris. "After the fight I was sitting in a booth when Corliss—that's the new Mrs. Nelson—came in on some business of her own and spotted me. She sensed how drunk I was. She figured I probably had a roll on me, a roll that I'd worked hard for. She knew I'd be clipped if I stayed where I was in my condition. So she played the good Samaritan. She waltzed me out of there, drove me down here in her own car, and had Wally put me to bed in a vacant cabin so I could sleep it off without some tart taking me."

Wally nodded. "That's right. Corliss is all the time doing nice things like that for sailors."

"Why?" the soft-spoken man asked him.

Wally shrugged. "Who can understand a woman? Can I? Can you? Maybe because her first husband was a sailor. A lieutenant commander, I understand. He went down with his submarine. It could be a memory, like, to him."

"I see," the man said. He looked back at me. "This Beachcomber is a dive?"

"I guess you would call it that."

"Then how come your wife happened to drop in?"

Wally leaned his fat palms on the bar. "Excuse I should say it, mister." He made certain there were no customers in the bar. "But that Wolkowysk was a sonofabitch. And Mrs. Nelson didn't just happen to drop into the Beachcomber. She went there to give Wolkowysk hell."

"What about?"

"On account of he was telling it all up and down the highway," he leaned over the bar and lowered his voice, "that she would do it for twenty dollars. Another guy had dropped in just that evening. And Corliss was sore as hell. When she left here she told me she was going to have a showdown with Wolkowysk and if he didn't promise to keep his dirty tongue off her she was going to Sheriff Cooper and have him put under peace bond or something."

The man asked, "What was Wolkowysk's grudge

against Mrs. Nelson? Why should he want to embarrass her?"

Wally told him. "On account of she went out with him once. To a dance in Manhattan Beach. For the cancer fund, see. And Wolkowysk got fresh coming home and she told him where to get off."

The man with Cooper and Harris drummed on the bar, then looked back at me. "And that's all you know about Wolkowysk?"

I lied, "That's all I know about Wolkowysk. Look. Who are you, fellow?"

He took his shield from his pocket and laid it on the wood. It read, "U.S. Federal Bureau of Investigation."

"The name," he said, "is Green. Lyle Green. Working out of the Los Angeles office at the moment."

Wally's eyes bugged. "Wadda you know about that? But why all the interest in Jerry Wolkowysk? So he had an accident. Why should the F.B.I. be interested in him? I thought he was just another petty punk. You know, like some bartenders are."

Harris horned in, trying to be important. "Ha. His name wasn't even Wolkowysk. It was Lippy Saltz. You know. That Chicago gambler who is mixed up in that Phillip E. Palmer business. The F.B.I. wanted him bad. For murder. They got proof now he scragged Palmer, using that red-haired stripper—what's her name, Sophia Palanka—as his come-on. Then him and her sail for Europe just as cool as you please, using Palmer's passport."

Green gave him a sour look.

Wally repeated, "Well, wadda ya know? I been reading

all about it in the papers. How the guy's body is found near Gary when all the time his family and the U. S. State Department, Atcheson even, think that Uncle Joe has lowered the boom on him. They do it for his money, eh?"

Green said, "A quarter of a million dollars."

I loosened the top button of my shirt. I poured myself a drink and drank it. The rum was so much water. Out of all the guys in the world who needed killing, I had to pick one who was wanted by the F.B.I.

Chapter Fourteen

Green lighted a cigarette. "A nasty affair all around. And not turning out at all as we had hoped. We were practically breathing down Saltz's neck. Now all we have is his wrecked car. We don't even know he's dead."

"How come?" Wally asked.

Sheriff Cooper said, "There was no body in the car."

I took a deep breath and held it. Corliss and I were in the clear. No one could prove anything. One of two things had happened: The tide had sucked Wolkowysk's body out of the car, or it had spilled out during the fall and been pounded to pulp on the rocks.

I poured another drink and the neck of the bottle rattled against the glass.

Harris touched my elbow. "What are you so nervous about, Nelson?"

I pushed back off the stool and faced him. "Why don't you leave me alone?"

"Cut it, you two," Cooper said.

Wally resumed drying glasses. "It was an accident?" he asked Green. "I mean, Saltz's car going over the cliff."

"I doubt it," Green said. "Did Wolkowysk ever bring a woman here?"

Wally thought a moment. "Not that I recall. You still haven't got a line on this Sophia Palanka, huh?"

Green said dryly, "That's something I'm not at liberty

to disclose. How many women live here permanently?"

"Two. Mrs. Nelson and Mrs. Meek."

"Are they blonde or brunette?"

"Mrs. Nelson is a blonde. Mrs. Meek is a brunette."

"Neither of them have red hair?"

"No, sir," Wally said.

"How old are they?"

"They're both in their early twenties."

Green looked at me. "I wonder if we could talk to Mrs. Nelson. It can just be that during their one date Wolkowysk told her something that might be of interest to us."

I said, "If you will wait until Corliss comes back from San Diego, I'm certain she'll be glad to talk to you."

Wally felt called upon to explain. "This is the day Mrs. Nelson does our buying from the wholesale houses."

"I see," Green said. "Mind if I ask you a few questions, Nelson?"

I said, "Not at all."

"What's Mrs. Nelson's exact age?"

"Twenty-three."

"Mr. Connors says she's a blonde."

"That's right."

"If you'll pardon the question, natural or artificial?"

"Natural."

"What's her background?"

I told him what Corliss had told me. "She was raised in a small town in the Midwest. When she was seventeen she married the local rich man's son. A naval officer. A lieutenant commander named John Mason. He was lost at sea. She used the money he left her to buy this court."

"Then she was really *Mrs*. Mason before she married you, a widow."

"That's right."

"How long have you been married?"

"Since the night before last."

"You knew each other before?"

"No."

"How long have you been stateside?"

"Three days."

He wasn't being nasty about it, just amused. "Rather a rapid courtship, wasn't it?"

"Sailors work fast," Harris said. "Especially when they spot an easy berth."

I got off the stool again, hot. "Another crack out of you and I'll push your teeth so far down your throat—"

"Yeah. I know," Harris broke in. "It'll take a Geiger counter to find them." He rested his hand on the waffled butt of the gun in his holster. "The times that I've been told that."

Sheriff Cooper lost his temper. "Goddamn. I told you two to cut it out. This is a murder investigation."

My head and throat began to ache again. I felt cold all over. I climbed back on the stool.

Green asked Sheriff Cooper, "What's Mrs. Nelson's reputation, Sheriff?"

Cooper formed a circle with his thumb and second finger. "A lady. She runs a clean court and an orderly bar and restaurant. I only wish we had more like her along the highway."

"How long has she owned the Purple Parrot?"

"Over two years."

"Three years next week," Wally corrected him. "I know, because I opened the bar for her. She put an ad in the San Diego paper and I answered it. It said, 'Wanted, experienced bar and restaurant man capable of taking full charge of first-class tourist-court restaurant and bar on Highway U.S. One-o-one. Drunks please save your time and mine.'" He beamed, proud of his feat of memory. "I remember it word for word on account of it's the best job I ever had. I get a salary plus a percentage of the gross. And like Sheriff Cooper says, Mrs. Nelson is a real lady."

Green snuffed his cigarette. "How about this Mrs. Meek?"

"She's nice, too," Wally said. "Mamie is a good girl and a hard worker." He confided, "But I don't think she's too happy with Meek."

Green was impatient with him. "How long has she been at the court?"

Wally thought a moment. "The Meeks have been here going on, or a little over, two years. Mrs. Nelson had to fire the two couples we had before them. One pair was just plain lazy. The other were a couple of lushes. Winos yet."

Cooper asked Green if he wanted to talk to Mrs. Meek.

"Later," Green said. "I'll want to talk to both women." He looked at me thoughtfully. "But right now we've got to get on into Palm Grove. I want the technicians' report on the car."

Green left with Cooper and Harris tagging at his heels. I sat staring after their backs. My throat still ached. My collar was still too tight. I fumbled at the top button of my shirt and found that it was open. I filled my glass. Then suddenly I didn't want it. I didn't like the way Green had looked at me. I didn't like the thought of his talking to Corliss. She might make one slip. One slip would be all he needed to make him pounce at her, ask her personal, embarrassing questions until she became hysterical and talked.

Then the whole thing would come out. And even if Jerry Wolkowysk had been Lippy Saltz, by disposing of the body I'd turned what I'd done into murder.

I sipped at the drink I didn't want, tugging at my collar, watching Wally towel glasses. His fat face shone with excitement as he talked on and on and on, like a half-witted parrot.

"Wadda you know? Wadda you know, huh?" he asked me. "That slimy stinker Wolkowysk turning out to be Lippy Saltz. The nerve of him. A guy like him making a play for a sweet girl like Mrs. Nelson."

I snarled at him. "Shut up."

The rinse water was running in the drain. Wally didn't hear me. He talked on.

"Why, if I'd known who the guy was, I'd a beat in his head with a bung starter. Instead of throwing him out on his tail. I'd a mashed him good. Then I'd a yelled for the cops. And maybe I'd a got a big reward, huh?"

It was hot in the bar. And still. I felt as if I were becalmed in the eye of a hurricane with not too distant winds building up to a blow. Then the bar stool began to revolve, faster and faster and faster.

"Hit him, Swede," Corliss had said. "Hit him as hard as you can."

I looked at my fist. I had. Then, instead of calling the cops, I'd disposed of the body, turning manslaughter into murder.

Wally started in again. "Boy. That Sophia Palanka dame must be some hot stuff, huh? I mean to get her hooks into a guy like Phillip E. Palmer the Third." He leaned across the bar and confided, "Maybe they're doing it even, huh? I mean when Lippy kills him."

I yelled at him. "I told you to shut up."

His fat baby-pink face turned red. "Why should I?"

"Because I said so."

He was as big as I was, with plenty of beef under his fat. He started to get sore, then changed his mind. "Just as you say, Mr. Nelson," he said meekly.

I stood up, gripping the lip of the bar. "Where can I contact Corliss?"

"That I wouldn't know, Mr. Nelson."

"You said this was her day to buy from the whole-salers."

"It is."

"What are their names?"

Wally shook his head. "Geez. She buys first one place, then another. I can give you a lot of names in Dago. But sometimes she even drives up to L.A. That's where I think she is now."

I grabbed him by the front of his shirt. "You're lying to me."

He protested, "Why should I lie to you, Mr. Nelson? If you want, I'll give you a stack of receipted bills. A foot high."

I released his shirt and sat back on the stool, then got

up again and walked to the front door. I was too jumpy to sit still. I *had* to talk to Corliss before Green did. I had to warn her what to expect, warn her to keep her mouth shut, no matter how Green pounded at her.

"Is something wrong?" Wally asked.

"No. Nothing at all," I told him. "I've been drinking too much, I guess."

I debated asking him to lend me his Ford so I could drive into Dago and look for Corliss. I decided it wouldn't be smart. San Diego is a big city. Three hundred and sixty-five thousand people live in it. I might drive down one street while Corliss drove down another and return to the court to find Green waiting. I didn't want that to happen. I wanted to be on deck when Green talked to her.

I corked the bottle I'd been working on and put it in my pocket. "I'm going over to the cottage. If Corliss should call here, tell her to call me. Tell her it's very important." I added, lamely. "I—I want her to bring me something from Dago."

"Yes, sir, Mr. Nelson," Wally said. "If Mrs. Nelson should call, I'll tell her."

He leaned a little too hard on the "Mr." I turned in the doorway and looked at him. His fat face was as sober as ever, but there was a certain quality to his voice that made it sound as if he was laughing. Inside. To himself.

I considered walking back and asking him what was so funny. But I'd met Wally's kind before. He looked soft but he wasn't. All it would mean was more trouble.

I walked out under the neon parrot and stood looking at the closed door of the office cottage. Now, with this new development, Mamie had said too much or not enough. I wanted another talk with her. Alone. A long talk.

I crunched across the gravel to the cottage. The screen door to the porch was hooked. I banged the wood. Then I rang the bell under the small metal plaque with the word "Manager" on it.

Meek opened the inside door. "Oh. It's you, Mr. Nelson," he said. He didn't move out of the doorway.

I rattled the screen door. "If it's not too much of an imposition, I'd like to talk to Mrs. Meek."

Meek acted embarrassed. "Could you come back a little later, Mr. Nelson?"

"No," I said flatly. "I want to talk to her right now."

"Well," he said. "Well." He crossed the porch and unhooked the screen. "In that case, come in, Mr. Nelson." He stepped aside to allow me to pass him. "I'll see if I can wake her up. But I don't know if I can."

All the cottages were the same, one big room with a bath, a porch, and a carport. Mamie was lying on an unmade bed, bare-legged, in her slip, snoring soddenly. Her slip rose and fell with her breathing. There was an empty gin bottle on the floor and a small vial of red capsules that looked like seconal on the table by the bed. Her breathing was labored. Her lips drew tight across her teeth, then blew out as she exhaled. Her face was slack and unattractive. All of her charm was gone. She was just another drunken dame.

"What's the idea?" I asked Meek.

He picked at the fuzz on his dirty sweater, nervously. "I'm sorry you should know about it, Mr. Nelson. But Mamie does this every once in a while."

"You mean, goes off on one?"

"Yeah." Meek tried to excuse her. "But only when she gets blue or depressed. And she was awfully blue about something this morning. She's been blue since last night, in fact."

"She didn't say about what?"

"No. She didn't." Meek wiped his nose on the back of his hand. "Then the next thing I knew, this had happened. You want me to see if I can wake her?" He shook her. "Mamie. Wake up. Mr. Nelson wants to talk to you."

Mamie snored on.

Meek started to shake her again.

"Don't bother," I told him. "Let her sleep."

He drew a sheet over her, tardily. "Just as you say, Mr. Nelson." He wiped his nose on his hand again. "And don't worry about Mamie's work. I can do hers as well as mine. I've done it before. Quite a few times."

There was a sour bilgelike smell about the cottage. I edged toward the door.

Meek followed me. "And if you please, Mr. Nelson, don't say anything to Mrs. Nelson. She fired the last couple she had for getting drunk. And Mamie and I like it here. We like the work."

I said I wouldn't say anything to Corliss.

"Thank you," Meek said. "Thank you a *lot,* Mr. Nelson."

He closed the door while I was still standing on the porch. I had the same feeling I'd had in the bar, that Meek was very amused by something.

I crossed the drive to Corliss' cottage. The blinds were closed. The one big room was dark and smelled of

Corliss. Without bothering to switch on the light, I lay down on the bed and waited. Thinking of a lot of things.

Love. A will-o'-the-wisp. St. Elmo's fire. A biological urge. The chemical affinity of one body for another. The deep-rooted urge of the male to propagate his kind. A package of cigarettes. A Hershey bar. A ten-thousand-dollar mink coat. Five dollars.

I was too jumpy to rest. I walked to the window and looked out. The late afternoon was gray. As I looked out the window the purple neon parrot perched on the roof of the bar winked on. Its beady eyes, veiled by wisps of fog, had a somehow evil, waiting look.

I took my wallet from my pocket and looked at the bus ticket to Hibbing.

For some reason I felt trapped.

Chapter Fifteen

At five I began to drink again. It was almost seven when Corliss returned. I heard her car purr into the port. Then she slipped in the side door and stood in the room with her back against the door.

I was still standing in the dark, the only illumination the light slanting in through the blinds from the spotlighted palms. The light formed silver bars across her face and chest. Corliss looked tired. From her chest down she was in darkness.

"What's the idea of standing there in the dark?" she asked me.

I asked her if she'd stopped at the bar.

"No," Corliss said. "I didn't. Why?"

I told her. "They've found Wolkowysk."

Her white face moved up and down behind the silver bars as she swallowed. "Who found him? Sheriff Cooper?"

"No. Two surf fishermen. That is, they found the car."

"But not his body?"

"No. The tide must have sucked it out."

Corliss pushed through the silver bars of light and sat on the edge of the bed. "How do you know?"

I said, "Sheriff Cooper was here. About three o'clock this afternoon."

Corliss took off her shoes. "He was?"

"Yeah."

"Was he suspicious? Did he seem to suspect you?"

"Us," I corrected her.

"Us, then." Corliss pulled at the toes of her stockings.

I said, "He didn't say. I think he was. They know he was in the bar that night. They know it wasn't an accident."

She laid back her coat. "Give me a cigarette. Please, Swede."

I lighted a cigarette and gave it to her.

Corliss sucked at it until its tip glowed like a miniature running light. "Well, not finding his body is a break. Even if they are suspicious, they can't do anything to us unless they find his body. Can they, Swede?"

I said, "I don't know. Maybe. Maybe not. But their finding Wolkowysk's car wasn't the worst of it."

"What do you mean?"

"There was an F.B.I. man with Cooper. A lad by the name of Green. Working out of L.A."

The bars of light were across her hair now, setting it on fire. All I could see was her hair, her forehead, and her eyes. The eye Wolkowysk had punched was still slightly swollen. There was fear in her eyes. "An F.B.I. man? Why should the F.B.I. be interested in Jerry Wolkowysk?"

I said, "It seems Jerry Wolkowysk was an alias. His right name was Lippy Saltz."

Corliss lighted the night light on the bed table. She looked small and worried and lovely. "Is that supposed to mean something to me?"

"You don't know the name?"

"No."

"Wolkowysk didn't tell you his right name was Saltz the one time you went out with him?"

"No."

"Did he tell you where he was from?"

"No."

"But you do read the newspapers?"

"Of course."

"Saltz was half of the murder team in that Phillip E. Palmer affair. In Chicago. He and a red-haired strip-teaser by the name of Sophia Palanka took Palmer for a quarter of a million dollars."

Corliss pulled at the toes of her stockings again. When she looked up she was breathing harder than she had been. Her lower lip thrust out. "I knew he was no good. Look what he did to me. I'm glad you killed him. You hear me, Swede? I'm glad you killed him."

I caught at her wrist. "For God's sake, not so loud."

"Well, I am."

"All right. So you are. Shut up. Let's keep it to our-selves."

Corliss screamed, "Don't yell at me."

I screamed back, "I'm not yelling."

I sat in an easy chair facing the bed. Corliss pulled her skirt up to her knees and unfastened her stockings. I looked away.

"What did you say the federal man's name was?" Corliss asked.

"Green. Lyle Green."

"And he and Cooper were here—when?"

"About three o'clock."

Corliss looked at her watch. "Are they coming back?"

"They said they were."

"What time?"

"They didn't say."

Corliss wriggled her bare toes in the loops of the white pile rug we'd bought to replace the one I'd burned. Then she squeezed her hair together with both hands and held it at the back of her neck.

"I'm scared, Swede."

"So am I."

She seemed glad to have company. "You are?"

"Yeah. I told you we shouldn't try to hide the body."

Corliss released her hair. "I know you did." She swallowed. "But I was just about as scared then as I am now. Did the federal man say he wanted to talk to me?"

"He wants to talk to both you and Mamie."

"Why?"

I quoted Green. "He said, 'It can just be that during their one date Wolkowysk told her something that might be of interest to us.'"

"But he didn't," Corliss protested. "He didn't tell me anything about himself. What else did he ask you?"

"What your background was."

"What did you tell him?"

"What you told me."

"Oh," Corliss said. "Oh." She squeezed her hair to the back of her neck again in a nervous gesture.

I said, "Then he asked Wally how old you and Mamie were and if you were blonde or brunette. Wally said Mamie was brunette and you were blonde. Then Green asked me if you were a natural or an artificial blonde. I told him natural."

One corner of Corliss' mouth turned down. "You ought to know." She stood up, pulled her dress over her head, and laid it across the back of a chair. All she was wearing under it was a garter belt and bra. "Well, there's no use sitting here crying in our beer. What's done is done." She padded barefooted to the dresser and began to comb her hair back, preparatory to tying it. "I'm going to take a quick shower. Then let's go up and eat. I'm starved."

She unhooked her bra and scratched where the strap had been. As she did, she dropped the comb. She stooped and picked it up.

I said, "Before you shower, come here a moment. Please."

Corliss padded back across the room and stood in front of me. "Again? Before we eat?"

I patted my face with my handkerchief. "Sit down. I want to talk to you."

Corliss sat on the edge of the bed. Then she fluffed a pillow and lay back, one knee raised and waving slightly, the way it had in Tijuana. "All right. Go ahead. I'm listening."

I leaned forward in the chair. "Why are Meek and Wally laughing at me? Why should Mamie tell me I'm in danger, that I'm being played for a fall guy?"

Corliss settled her head more comfortably on the pillow. "I haven't the least idea what you're talking about." Her eyes narrowed. "Are you drunk again, Swede?"

I said, "I've been drinking. But don't try to change the subject."

Corliss said, "I'm not trying to change the subject. You made a statement. I told you I didn't know what you were talking about. I can also tell you I'm not going to put up with this constant drinking. I won't. I can't."

"Maybe I have reason to drink."

"Staying drunk won't bring Wolkowysk back to life."

"I wasn't thinking of Wolkowysk."

"What then?"

"You."

She snuggled down on the pillow. "Well, if we're going to, let's get it over."

"I thought you had to have love with yours."

Corliss said, "Oh, for God's sake." Exasperated. "Are we a couple of kids in the back seat of a car, or what?" She moved to the edge of the bed and started to get up.

I pushed her back. "I said I wanted to talk to you."

She folded the spread over her thighs. "You're crazy, Swede. You must be."

"Why?"

"You've acted like an entirely different man ever since we've been married."

"Maybe I have a reason."

"What?"

I gave it to her cold turkey. "Are you certain that Wolkowysk *forced* you? Or was it something else?"

Corliss panted, "You're crazy."

"You said that before."

"I mean it."

I'd had all afternoon and all the night before to think. "All right. Then tell me this."

"What?"

"How come Wolkowysk's clothes were folded so neatly on that chair? Why did he spit in your face? Why did he call you a bitch? Why did he say, 'You would'? Are you sure he wasn't in your bed by invitation?" I grabbed her bare shoulders and shook her. "Answer me."

Corliss twisted out of my hands. She crawled to the head of the bed and sat with her back to the wall. "You're mad. You're out of your mind, Swede."

I moved over on the bed with her. She sat even straighter against the headboard. "And tell me this. Why were you so frightened of that drunk in Tijuana? If you couldn't understand what he was saying, how do you know he was insulting you? Are you certain that background data you gave me is correct? Are you certain you bought this court with money your first husband left you?"

Corliss had difficulty in breathing. "How else could I buy it?"

I told her. "There's one sure way a girl with your looks can make money. A hundred dollars a night. Almost any amount she names."

Corliss ran her hands over her breasts. "And that's what you think I am?"

"At least I'm beginning to wonder."

"Why?" Corliss said. "Why do you think so?"

"The way you act."

"How do I act?"

I told her. "Like every tart I've ever known. Unless you're unnaturally aroused, you have the same look in your eyes. The same forced smile. You make the same forced response. You're a lady until you take off your clothes. The minute they're off, you revert to type." I mimicked a water-front blister. " 'Hello, sailor. Lonely?' " That's what they all say. Is that why Wally and Meek are laughing at me? What have I got into?"

Corliss kicked at me with her bare heels. "I won't be talked to like that. I won't be." She began to cry, hysterically. "Take the car. Take anything you want. But get out of here. Get out of my life. Let's call it quits. Right now. Tonight."

I gripped one of the bare feet kicking at me and pulled her down on the bed until I could bend and kiss her without moving.

"That's the hell of it, baby. I can't."

Corliss' voice was muffled under my lips. "Why can't you?"

"For two reasons. One, I love you."

"Love!"

I held her squirming body firmly. "Then there's Wolkowysk, or Lippy Saltz, or whatever you want to call him." I pressed my cheek against her hair. "Green wants to talk to me again. He wants to talk to you. We're tied together now. For life. We don't dare leave each other."

The sweetness of her hair, the heat and softness of her flesh excited me. I fondled her.

"Oh, Swede. Swede, my darling," Corliss sobbed. She responded frenziedly. But only for a moment. Then she squirmed away and stood in the narrow space between the bed and the wall.

Her lower lip thrust out. Her eyes were sullen. She

was breathing so hard it was difficult for her to talk.

"No. I'm a—what you called me. I charge a hundred dollars a night. Now leave me alone until I'm showered and dressed. When I am, we're going up to the bar and get some food in you." Her eyes filled and spilled over. Tears trickled down her cheeks. "Then maybe I can make you understand what you've just done to me."

Chapter Sixteen

I was near the sea. I could smell it. Not that it made any difference. Corliss had called it quits. We were through.

It hurt to move. My muscles felt as if they'd been pounded with a chipping hammer. My eyes were swollen shut and sealed with mucus. I'd taken a hell of a beating from someone.

I lay waiting for the bunk to stop rocking.

"You can't talk to me like that, Swede. No man can. I won't put up with it for one minute. Take the car. Take whatever you want. But you and I are through. I don't want to ever see you again."

That had been in the bar, in a booth, with Corliss sitting opposite me, looking cool and fresh and virginal in white, eating prime ribs au jus, urging me to eat; me unable to eat, nursing a fresh bottle of Bacardi.

It began to come back clearer. Both of us had been jumpy, waiting for Green and Sheriff Cooper to show. Corliss had asked if I wanted my rings back. I'd told her not to talk like a fool, that whatever either she or I was, it was us, Swede and Corliss, from now on. Then what?

I sat up on the edge of the bunk and opened one eye, cautiously. The first thing I saw was vitreous china, a washbasin, and a stool without a seat. I was in a four-by-seven cubicle. Three sides of the cubicle were solid steel. There were bars on the fourth side.

I looked through the bars and saw a good-looking colored lad in a cell across the way watching me with interest. "You snapped out of it, huh?" he asked. "You lay so still I thought you were dead."

I stood up and found my cap on the top bunk. "Where am I?"

The question amused him. "You're in jail, sailor. In the San Mateo County Jail."

I considered the information. The San Mateo County line was ninety miles up the coast from the Purple Parrot. And the last thing I remembered was sitting in a booth in the bar with Corliss.

"You wouldn't have a cigarette, would you, fellow?" I asked the lad across the way.

He said, "I wish I had."

I gripped the bars. "Do I look nuts to you?"

He debated a long time. "N-no," he decided finally. "You're so beaten up it's hard to tell what you look like. But I wouldn't say you weren't in your right mind. You look sane enough to me."

"Were you here when they brought me in? Do you know what I'm charged with?"

He shook his head. "No. You were pounding your ear when they brought me in. But you should have a property receipt, and the charge against you will be listed on that."

I went through my pockets and found the receipt in my shirt. It read:

Department of Public Safety
DIVISION OF POLICE
San Mateo County, California

DATE   *6-20-51*   TIME *1:10*   CELL NO.   *7*
NAME   *Nelson (NMN) Swen*
ALIAS
ADDRESS *1001 Ocean Drive, Palm Grove, Calif.*
       (U.S. 101)
AGE   *33*   DESCENT   *Scandinavian*
           OCCUPATION *Seaman*
HEIGHT *6'2"* WEIGHT *225*   BUILD *Husky*
       HAIR   *Yellow* EYES   *Blue*
OFFENSE   *V.C. 502-148 P.C.*
WHERE ARRESTED   *Topanga Canyon*
ARRESTED BY   *Thomas & Morton*
SEARCHED BY   *T. N. Thompson*

I asked the lad across the way if he knew what V.C. 502 and 148 P.C. meant.

"You have me there, sailor," he admitted.

"V.C. Five-o-two," a sleepy voice from the cell next to mine informed me, "is driving while intoxicated. One-four-eight P.C. is resisting an officer. You woke me up once at two o'clock, still resisting very cheerfully at the top of your goddamn voice. Now it's five o'clock in the morning. For God's sake, shut your big mouth and let the rest of us get some sleep."

I laid the receipt on the bunk and washed my face and head with cold water. The water stung the cuts and contusions, but it made me feel a lot better.

I picked up the receipt again and read on.

PROPERTY RECEIPT

1 belt — 2 pks. cigarettes
1 bottle rum (Bacardi)
1 wrist watch (Lord Elgin)
1 diamond ring (lady's — approx. 2 carats)
1 wallet — seaman's papers

CURRENCY $11,925   SILVER $4.21
    TOTAL $11,929.21

CAR MAKE   *Cadillac*   COLOR   *Green*
TYPE   *Con. coupe Ser. 62, '51*
PRESENT LOCATION *Police garage*   LIC. NO. *8824N*

I folded the receipt carefully, put it in my pocket, then washed my face with cold water again.

What was I doing with Corliss' ring and car? What was I doing in San Mateo? I *had* to be with Corliss when Green questioned her. One slip of her tongue, one moment of hysteria could mean the gas chamber for me.

There was the hollow bang of an opened steel door in the distance. Feet scuffed down the cement. A uniformed officer peered in through the bars of my cell.

"You come to yet, Nelson?"

I gripped the bars. "And perfectly cold sober. Look, Jack. How are the chances of speaking to the officers who arrested me?"

He unlocked the door of my cell. "As it happens, they're good. Straight down the corridor, Nelson. To where you see that open door."

There was a second officer standing in the open

doorway. When I reached him he snapped a pair of hand-cuffs on my wrists. "Just a matter of precaution."

I said, "I'm not going to run away."

"I know you're not," he assured me. He walked behind me, dangling a sap from his wrist. "Just keep on going until you come to a door with 'Captain of Detectives' printed on the glass."

When I came to the door I opened it and walked in.

A pleasant-faced white-haired man was sitting back of a desk talking to a younger man. The faces of the two uniformed policemen standing against the wall were vaguely familiar.

"Not so tough now, eh, Nelson?" one of them asked.

The white-haired man introduced himself. "I'm Captain Marks." He nodded at the younger man. "This is Assistant District Attorney Flagle. I believe you've met officers Morton and Thomas."

I looked at the cops standing against the wall. If they were the officers I'd resisted, they were good at their trade. Neither of them had a mark.

Flagle motioned me to a chair. "Feeling pretty rocky?"

I realized I was wearing my cap and took it off. "That's right."

"Give him a drink," Flagle said. "A good stiff drink."

The white-haired man who'd said his name was Captain Marks took a bottle of bonded whisky from the bottom drawer of his desk. He poured a water glass a quarter full and handed it to me.

I drank it and returned the glass. "Thanks."

"Some water?"

"No. That will do fine."

The whisky spread out in my stomach in little warming fingers. I didn't feel too bad. I balanced my white cap on my knee and waited, wary. Whenever a cop buys you a drink, especially in a station house, he wants something in return.

Still friendly, Flagle said, "Been on a bit of a bender, eh, Nelson?"

"So it would seem," I admitted.

The whisky glow began to fade. Captains of detectives and assistant district attorneys didn't climb out of bed before dawn to put drunken drivers through the mill. There was only one thing it could be. Green had questioned Corliss. Corliss had got hysterical and talked.

Still, that didn't explain what I was doing with her car and ring ninety miles up the coast from the Purple Parrot.

Captain Marks fingered some papers on his desk. "Is this address correct, Nelson? You live at Ten-o-one Ocean Drive in Palm Grove?"

"Yes, sir."

He said, "That's rather an unusual address. Just what sort of place is it, Nelson?"

I said, "A twenty-unit motor court, restaurant, and bar called the Purple Parrot."

Flagle took a package of cigarettes from his pocket. I hoped he would offer me one. He didn't. "The Purple Parrot, eh? That's rather an attractive name for a court. You own this court, Nelson?"

I shook my head, and wished I hadn't, "No, sir. My wife owns it."

"Mrs. Swen Nelson."

"That's right."

Flagle lighted a cigarette and looked at me as if I were a slug of some kind. All four men felt the same way about me. I could sense it. To them I was so much dirt.

I stood the silence as long as I could. The walls of the office seemed to be closing in. I'd had the same feeling before. Down twenty fathom in diving dress, with my air hose fouled. "Look," I said. "What's this all about? What's the charge? You fellows aren't going to believe this, but I haven't the least idea how I got up here from the Purple Parrot. The last I remember, I was sitting in a booth in the bar, drinking supper with my wife."

"Don't try to be funny," Flagle said.

"I'm not trying to be funny," I said.

Captain Marks laid a gun on his desk blotter. "Ever see this gun before, Nelson?"

I breathed a little easier. I hadn't killed Wolkowysk with a gun. I'd made certain his gun, a .45 Colt automatic, had been in the pocket of his coat when I'd helped him drive over the cliff. This was a little peashooter, a pearl-handled .25 similar to the one Corliss kept in her top dresser drawer. I hedged. "I've seen a lot of guns like that. Why? Should I have seen that particular gun before?"

Marks thumbed the safety on and off and on again. "An efficient and a very deadly little weapon."

I had to know. "Where did you get it? What has it to do with me?"

Marks said coldly, "We found it in the glove compartment of the car you were driving when Officers Morton and Thomas arrested you. A green convertible Cadillac coupé, registered in the name of Corliss Mason." Marks tapped the gun with a pencil. "Fired recently. Only one shell left in the clip." He walked around his desk and leaned against it, facing me. "All right. Let's stop beating around the bush. Where is she, Nelson?"

"Where is who?"

"Mrs. Nelson."

Sweat escaped from the roots of my hair. "Why, she's home. Back at the Purple Parrot. I suppose."

"He supposes," Flagle said.

Marks doubled his fist and hit me on the side of the head, his clenched knuckles up, the back of his hand parallel with the floor. "You lying sonofabitch."

The blow sent me sprawling on all fours, I scrambled to my feet and the two cops stepped away from the wall.

"Sit down," one of them said.

I sat back in the chair.

There was a brown paper bundle on the desk, tied with string. Flagle broke the string and took out a blood-stained white dress, a white satin bra, a pair of panties, a garter belt, and a pair of silver sandals. The white panties were unspotted, but the garter belt and the bra were as stained with blood as the dress. The dress looked like the one Corliss had slipped into after our quarrel in the cottage.

Flagle dug in the paper again and added a white leather purse initialed with a silver C and M to the small pile of clothing on the desk. "Care to identify any of these, Nelson?" he asked me.

A lump formed in my throat. Almost too big to swallow. My voice had to squeeze around it. "They look like my wife's clothes. Where is she? What's happened to Corliss?"

I got to my feet again.

"Sit down," Flagle said.

I sat down.

Captain Marks drummed on his desk with his fingertips. "You see, Nelson, when the boys picked you up this morning you were carrying a lot of money. Sergeant Brewer thought it might be worth the price of a phone call to do a little checking on you."

"So?"

"So he called down the coast to Sheriff Cooper of the Palm Grove police, and what Cooper told him was so interesting that Brewer sent the boys back to the police garage to give the car you were driving a thorough check." He touched the objects as he named them. "They found this gun in the glove compartment. This clothing and this purse were in the trunk." Marks tried to light the dead cigar he was chewing. It was so wet the match spluttered. He looked over the match at me. "Sheriff Cooper says you and Mrs. Nelson had a little quarrel last night. Is that so?"

I realized I was sitting on the edge of the chair, gripping my knees. I sat back and tried to relax. "Yes. It is. But—"

"What did you quarrel about, Nelson?"

I was damned if I'd tell him. "That's none of your business."

"Did Mrs. Nelson tell you she was through with you, ask you to get out?"

I said, "Yes, but—"

"But what?"

The bloodstained clothes on the desk, Corliss' remembered white face, Wolkowysk, who wasn't Wolkowysk at all but a killer by the name of Lippy Saltz for whom the F.B.I. was looking, all suddenly churned in my stomach. Like a ship's screw out of water. Faster and faster and faster. I gripped the sides of the chair.

"If you're going to be sick," Flagle said, "use the basin."

I did. For a long time. Then I filled my hands with cold water and buried my hot face in them.

Captain Marks beat at my back with his flat voice. "Is it also true that at the completion of this quarrel with your wife—during which, incidentally, according to Sheriff Cooper, she was naked except for a garter belt—you attempted to force her to have relations with you?"

I looked over my shoulder at him. "Who told Cooper that?"

Captain Marks said, "The gardener. A man named Meek. As I get the story, Meek is the nosy type and was watching you through a crack between the sill and the Venetian blind."

I turned and leaned against the basin, water dripping from my face. "What happened then?"

"You don't know?"

"I remember Corliss dressing. I remember walking over to the bar with her. I remember trying to eat and not being able to."

"So you drank some more instead."

"That's right."

"How long have you been drinking heavily, Nelson?"

"This is the third or fourth day."

"You don't remember leaving the Purple Parrot with Mrs. Nelson?"

"No."

"You don't remember getting into her car with her?"

"No."

"Well, you did. And neither of you were seen again until Officers Thomas and Morton crowded you off the road five hours later. You roaring drunk, offering to fight every sonofabitch cop in California."

I looked at Thomas and Morton. "You guys beat me up?"

The younger of the pair shook his head. "Naw. By the time we picked you up you were swinging at air, mate. You made a couple of passes at me and fell flat on your face. Not that you didn't give us plenty of trouble. You did. You fought every inch of the way to the car. Then when Bill got you in the back seat, you damn near kicked my head off."

Flagle picked up the bloodstained dress and dangled it in front of me. "What did you do with her, Nelson?"

I shook my head at him. "I don't know what you're talking about."

His smile was thin. "I think you do. For three days you've been leading the life of Reilly. A sailor's dream. Free booze. Free eats. A woman. You wanted it to go on forever. You hoped it would." He sunk the knife. "Then when Mrs. Nelson smarted up and told you she was through, you lost your head and killed her."

I shouted, "That's a lie! Corliss isn't dead. She can't be dead. Where is she?"

"That," Captain Marks said quietly, "is what we want you to tell us. Start talking, Nelson. What did you do with her body?"

Chapter Seventeen

The day had been hot and long. A lot of things had happened. Most of them to me. None of them nice. The night wind blowing in the windows of the car felt good.

Captain Marks turned around in the front seat. "Say when, Nelson."

I said, "It's the next tourist court on the left side of the road. Just before you come to the hill. Where you see those spotlighted palms."

The driver of the San Mateo squad car hand-signaled to the cars behind us and pulled in in front of the bar. Several men were clustered in the dark under the unlighted neon parrot.

Captain Marks got out of the car. "Which of you gentlemen is Sheriff Cooper?"

Cooper detached himself from the group of waiting men. "I'm Cooper. Captain Marks of San Mateo?"

"That's right," Marks said. They shook hands.

I sat looking at the handcuffs on my wrists. The police cars behind the one in which I was riding swung in off the highway. Uniformed and plain-clothes men got out and joined the group under the parrot. They shook hands. They leaned against the wall and Wally's Ford, talking earnestly, about me. Big men, little men, fat men, thin men—the law.

It was too dark for me to see their faces, but now and

then I could isolate snatches of conversation. One of them, it sounded like Flagle, brought up the matter of jurisdiction.

"Forget it," Sheriff Cooper said. "It will be time enough to worry about that when we find the body."

Deputy Sheriff Harris walked over to the car and looked in at me. "I knew you were a no-good bastard the first time I saw you."

I said, "You sonofabitch," and tried to get out of the car.

One of the two San Mateo detectives sitting beside me wrestled me back against the cushion. "Take it easy now, Nelson. Don't blow your top."

There was grit in my eyes. They burned from lack of sleep. Corliss was dead. I'd killed her. A dozen men working in shifts had hammered it into me all day. Now they told me to take it easy.

Captain Marks walked into the bar with Sheriff Cooper. In the doorway he turned and called, "O.K., boys. Bring Nelson in here."

One of the detectives asked me, "Are you going to walk, or do we carry you, Nelson?"

I said I'd walk. I walked between them to the door. There were no customers in the bar. Wally was standing in back of the wood. Meek was sitting on a bar stool. Cora, the heavy-set waitress, was crying at one of the tables.

Wally gave me a sour look. Meek wiped his nose on the back of his hand. Cora cried even harder. The bar wasn't friendly or wholesome now. It reminded me of the night before Corliss and I had been married. With terse whispers crawling the length of the wood like so many excited cockroaches.

Captain Marks stopped me halfway down the bar and asked Sheriff Cooper if he had checked on Mrs. Nelson's clothes.

Cooper said, "As soon as you phoned the request. That is, I had Mrs. Gilly do it."

Meek wiped the back of his hand on his pants. "My wife, Mamie, would have done it, but she's sick."

Captain Marks sat at the table across from Cora. "You're Mrs. Gilly?"

"Yes, sir."

"You're familiar with Mrs. Nelson's wardrobe?" Cora wiped her eyes with her handkerchief. "Fairly well, sir. And I'd say nothing is missing but Corliss' camel's-hair coat, the white silk shantung dress she was wearing when she ate supper, a pair of silver sandals, and a big white leather purse with a silver C and M on it."

One of the San Mateo detectives was carrying a battered director's case. He opened it on the bar, took out the bloodstained dress, and handed it to Captain Marks. Marks showed the dress to Cora. "Is this the dress Mrs. Nelson was wearing, Mrs. Gilly?"

Cora examined the top of the dress carefully. "Yes, sir. I remember noticing one of the shoulder straps needed tacking. See? There. I meant to tell Corliss about it. But everything was so upset."

"In what way?"

Cora looked at me, then away. "Well, Mr. Nelson was drinking so heavily and Corliss was crying and telling him she never wanted to see him again, begging him to get out."

Wally leaned his weight on the bar. "Why did you kill her, Nelson? Corliss never done you nothing but good."

Flagle sat on one of the bar stools. "Had Nelson been drinking all evening?"

Wally hooted. "All evening? The guy has been stewed for four days. His pockets were dipping sand when he showed up, and he's been drunk ever since." Wally added, earnestly, "You wouldn't believe me, mister, if I told you how much rum he put away."

Captain Marks bit the end from a cigar, "When they left here, who was driving?"

"She was," Wally said. "Nelson had just passed out on the table, see? I had to help Corliss put him in the car."

"Did she say where she was taking him?"

Wally spread his fat palms on the bar. "Not to me, mister. I just work here. I did have the impression, though, that she was going to drop him somewhere. You know, maybe in some hotel. Anyway, away from here." He confided, "You know yourself you can't have drunks passing out on the tables and falling all over the floor. Not in a respectable bar. We have mostly tourist trade. And most of the tourists have children."

I caught at a small straw bobbing on white water. I said, "I don't see how I was physically capable of killing her if I was so drunk I passed out on the table and Wally had to help put me in the car."

Flagle asked sarcastically, "It is your contention, then, that Mrs. Nelson is still alive? That having left her clothes and a considerable amount of blood in the back seat of her car, she is wandering around in her stockings and a camel's-hair coat, has been for twenty-four hours?"

I said, "I don't know where she is."

Harris asked Captain Marks if the San Mateo technicians had run a paraffin test on my hand.

Marks lighted his cigar. "Yeah. And it came out positive. The test on his right hand proved conclusively that Nelson fired a gun shortly before he was picked up. What's more, they found a couple of good prints on the clip."

I looked at my right hand. They said it had fired a gun. They said the paraffin test had brought out specks of burned powder.

Captain Marks got up from the table and leaned against the bar, talking to Sheriff Cooper. "The way we see it, he killed her around eleven o'clock last night. The crystal on his watch was smashed and the watch stopped at five minutes of eleven. What time did they leave here?"

Cooper said, "I'd judge a little before eight. I dropped in to ask Mrs. Nelson a few questions on another matter a few minutes after eight and Connors told me they'd just left."

Marks built his case against me. "She probably parked somewhere along the road to let him sober up a bit before she checked him into a hotel. Nelson came to and got nasty. She put up a hell of a fight. Maybe batted him around with a tire iron or something. That's where he got those scratches and bruises. Or maybe she used the butt of the gun. He wrestled it out of her hand and shot her." He pushed his hat back on his head. "But we're damned if we can figure what he did with the body. Unless he weighted it down and threw it in the ocean. In that case, it may be days, even weeks, before she's washed up on some beach."

"You say there was considerable blood in the car?"

"A lot of it. Type B, Rh positive."

Cooper bobbed his head. Like an old gray rooster pecking corn. "That would seem to do it. I checked with the mobile Red Cross blood bank this afternoon. A fine woman, Mrs. Nelson. She gave blood every ten weeks."

Flagle turned me around so my back was to the bar. "How about that, Nelson? After hearing that, do you still insist you didn't kill your wife?"

I tried to breathe normally. "If I did, I don't remember it. All I remember is quarreling with her."

"What did you quarrel about?"

I gave him the last part. "She wanted to call it quits. She told me to get out of her life."

Meek ran his coated tongue over his thin upper lip. "I seen you. I seen you through the blinds, trying to make her do it. You tried to force her and Corliss had to kick you in the face with her bare feet."

All the men in the bar looked at me as if I was dirt. I tried to find one friendly face. I couldn't. Then I saw Green, the man from the F.B.I. He was sitting on a stool at the far end of the bar, where Wolkowysk had sat. He looked detached, unbiased, just listening.

Flagle asked, "What else did Mrs. Nelson say?"

I told him the truth. "She said she wouldn't be talked to the way I'd been talking to her. She told me to take the car, take anything I wanted, but get out."

"Why didn't you?"

"Because I loved her."

"Love her," Wally sneered.

Flagle said, "You say she said she wouldn't stand for

the way you had been talking to her. How had you been talking to her?"

I felt the way I had while I'd waited for Corliss to come back from San Diego. I felt trapped. "I called her a tart."

"Why?"

"Because she acted like one."

Flagle took off his hat and ran his fingers through his hair. "I see. And after you'd called her that she told you to take her five-thousand-dollar Cadillac and anything else you wanted and get out."

It sounded silly when he said it.

"I suppose she forced her ring on you, too?"

"She asked if I wanted it back."

"How about the eleven thousand dollars you had in your pocket when you were arrested?"

"The money was mine."

Flagle lifted one eyebrow, amused. "Where did you get eleven thousand dollars?"

I told him. "I had twelve thousand on me when I came ashore. I'd saved my pay for three years."

"Why?"

"I intended to buy a farm. Near Hibbing Minnesota. Where I was born. I was going to get married and settle down."

Flagle drew his hand across his mouth. He didn't need to say it. I knew what he was thinking. Now he'd heard it all. He turned away from me. "Well, let's get on with it. I want to see the unit they occupied."

The bar and the restaurant were closed, but Meek was still renting cottages. A middle-aged couple was standing outside of Cottage Number 4 beside a green Chrysler with Illinois license plates. As we started across the court I heard the woman whisper, "Go on, Joe. Tell them what we saw when we drove in last night."

"No," the man said flatly.

Inside the cottage, Flagle fingered through the dresses in the closet. "You're certain nothing is missing, Mrs. Gilly?"

"Positive," Cora said. "Well, almost positive." She stroked one of Corliss' evening gowns. "Mrs. Nelson didn't go away willingly. I know that much. No woman would just walk out and leave all these beautiful clothes."

"No," Flagle agreed with her. "At least, it's very unlikely."

A bright bit of metal under the edge of the bed caught my eye. I stood leaning against the wall, wondering what it was.

Sheriff Cooper took a fat manila envelope from his pocket and handed it to Flagle. "These are the papers we took from the safe, Mr. Prosecutor. Connors had the combination."

"Was there any money in the safe?" Flagle asked him.

"Seven hundred and eighty dollars," Cooper said.

Wally had accompanied us to the cottage. Flagle asked him if I had the combination to the safe. Wally shook his head. "Uh-uh. Just me and Mrs. Nelson."

"He didn't have access to the safe at any time?"

"No, sir."

Flagle sorted through the papers in the manila envelope. They were mainly statements of record, a deed to the court, fire and wind and liability insurance policies, and receipted bills. "No will, eh?"

"I couldn't find one," Sheriff Cooper said.

Captain Marks said, "I doubt Nelson was thinking that far ahead. As I see it, the money is secondary. Nelson had a good thing. He knew it. He wanted to hang onto it. And when the girl told him she was through, he lost his head."

Finished with the papers in the envelope, Flagle dumped the contents of Corliss' white purse on the dresser and pushed the various items around on the glass. Pleased, he straightened out and held up a crumpled rectangle of white paper. "This is it."

Captain Marks got up to look at it. It was a safe-deposit bank form. The kind you have to fill out when you want to get in your box. Corliss had dated it wrong, scratched out the date, then, evidently, crumpled it into her purse and filled out another form.

Flagle asked Wally if Corliss had a safe-deposit box in San Diego.

"Yeah. I think she did," Wally said. "In fact, I know she did. Because once when we had a chance to get a good buy in whisky if we took fifty cases and paid cash, she said she didn't have that much in her checking account at the moment, but if the salesman would wait she would drive into Dago and get the money from her box. And she did."

Meek whined from the doorway, "So she got some more this afternoon. And you took it off her, huh, Nelson?"

Wally was fair. "No. I'm not standing up for Nelson, see? But right is right. And I don't think he took no money off Corliss."

"Why not?" Flagle asked him.

Wally said, "Because the first night he showed up I take his dough away from him for safekeeping. And he's loaded. He has fourteen thousand, eight hundred and seventy-five dollars on him."

"I seem," Flagle said sourly, "to have chosen the wrong profession."

My coat was as wet with sweat as it had been the night I killed Wolkowysk. I tried to make them understand. "Look, gentlemen. Something is very wrong here. I don't think Corliss is dead. If she is, I didn't kill her. I know."

"How do you know?" Flagle asked.

"Because I couldn't do such a thing. No matter how drunk I was. I couldn't kill a woman."

"You don't know what you could or couldn't do," Flagle said. "Your type of man doesn't know the meaning of normalcy, Nelson. You live for thrills, one emotional aphrodisiac piled on top of another. By your own admission you've had master's papers for years, but you prefer to sail as first mate to avoid responsibility. You've been a deep-sea diver. You've hunted diamonds in Africa while other men had to keep their noses to a desk or a workbench. All your life you've done just as you pleased. You've poked your nose into all the odd corners of the world. You've been a soldier of fortune. You've risked your life time after time—for a thrill. And this time you went too far."

Flagle paced the floor of the cottage, then stopped in front of me again.

"Look at it as a jury will see it. Your ship berthed four days ago. You say you bought a bus ticket for Hibbing, Minnesota. You say you intended to buy a farm and get married and settle down. We know you went on a drunk. We know you got in a crap game at the Beachcomber. We know you hit a man named Corado so hard you almost killed him. We know Mrs. Nelson, Mrs. Mason then, took pity on you and brought you here to her own court for safekeeping. You're big, good-looking, virile. Corliss Mason, a young widow, with all a young woman's normal passion and desire, became infatuated with you. You wanted a woman, by then a particular woman. But there was only one way you could have the particular woman you wanted. Somehow you persuaded Corliss Mason to marry you. But did you behave as a normal bridegroom might be expected to behave? No. After you got what you wanted, you went right on with your drunk, submitting her to God knows what indignities. You stayed sodden drunk for three days. Then when she realized what a heel you were and told you to get out, you stripped her and abused her. Then you killed her and hid her body."

"That's a lie."

I brought up my manacled hands. The chain caught Flagle under the chin, snapping his head back.

Then Harris took a quick step forward and hit me. Back of my left ear. With a blackjack. Panting, "You bastard. You lousy Swede bastard."

The blow knocked me to my knees, then flat on the deck. My cap rolled under the bed. The metal object I'd noticed before was less than an inch from my eyes.

Captain Marks' voice was a great surge of sound beating at me like breakers against a coral reef.

"We've had enough trouble with you, Nelson. Start talking. What did you do with your wife's body?"

I lay looking at the metal object.

Corliss was dead. The assumption was that I'd killed her. The law said we had left the Purple Parrot together, in her car, and neither of us had been seen again until Officers Thomas and Morton had curbed me in San Mateo, roaring drunk, offering to fight every cop in California.

Corliss hadn't returned to the Purple Parrot. She hadn't been seen since she had left with me.

Then what was her wedding ring, slightly too large for her finger, doing almost lost in the white loop pile of the new rug we'd bought to replace the one on which Lippy Saltz, alias Jerry Wolkowysk, had died?

Chapter Eighteen

I looked at the ring for a long time. It had been on Corliss' finger, under the engagement ring, while she'd been eating in the bar. I remembered seeing it, distinctly. From time to time Corliss had twisted it around on her finger as she talked.

"As long as you feel the way you do about me, you can't really love me. So let's call it quits. Maybe next time we'll both do better."

Her cheeks wet with tears. Between bites of prime ribs au jus. With no mention of Wolkowysk.

My cap had rolled under the bed. I reached for it and picked up the ring at the same time, tucking it under the sweatband of the cap. Showing the ring to Flagle, Marks, or Cooper wouldn't get me a thing. They *knew* I'd killed Corliss. So it was her wedding ring. I couldn't prove she'd been wearing it when we'd left the Purple Parrot. But she had. And sometime after she'd driven away with me Corliss had returned to the cottage.

Captain Marks helped me to my feet. "How about it, Nelson? Are you going to talk or do we have to turn on the heat?"

"O.K.," I lied. "I killed her. I'll tell you what."

"What?" Flagle asked flatly.

I bargained. "I'll trade you a full confession and the

body for permission to take a shower and put on a clean uniform."

Flagle nodded. "That's a deal. Now you're being sensible, Nelson. What did you do with the body?"

I held out my manacled hands. "Uh-uh. Not so fast. First the shower and the change of clothes."

Marks detailed one of his men to guard me. As I soaped myself I studied the purple and green bruises on my thighs, my abdomen, my arms. I hadn't taken a beating. I'd been worked over. My body looked as if someone had used a tire iron on it, enjoying what she was doing. A bee. A man. What was the difference? Only wings.

Out in the living bay, still cool and detached, Green joined the conversation. "So you've cracked your case, gentlemen."

"That's right," Captain Marks said, pleased. He laughed. "A bath for a confession and a body. Nelson must like to be clean."

"Yes. He must," Green said.

Flagle asked him if there was anything new on the Lippy Saltz affair.

"No. Not as yet," Green said. "But I think there may be some developments before the night is over."

Here in the night-filled hills rising sheer from the coast highway the only sounds were the crackling of brush and the heavy breathing of the long line of men behind me.

"How much farther?" Captain Marks asked.

"Not far now," I lied. "On top of the next hill, then across a flat space. What do you call them?"

166

"A plateau?"

"Yeah. That's right. A plateau."

Flagle asked, "What gave you the idea of hiding the body in a cave, Nelson?"

I said, "I came here once with a girl." That much was true. "We had a picnic."

"I'll bet you did," Harris said.

I quit the narrow trail through the greasewood and heather and cut across a rock fall to make the going tougher. Captain Marks had unlocked one of the cuffs before we started to climb. It jangled with every step. I experimented by putting the cuff in my coat pocket, but it was almost impossible to climb with only one hand.

Behind me, Flagle said, "The time element checks. It's been an hour and forty minutes since we left the Purple Parrot. But where are we?"

"I'll be damned if I know," Marks said.

Sheriff Cooper knew his coastline. "Back of Malibu, I think. Yes. I'm positive we are. Judging by the stars, we've been angling north and west since we left Topanga Canyon. As I recall, the highway is just the other side of this ridge. At the foot of a steep cliff."

"Oh, yes," Flagle grunted. "Of course. Where the highway department had all that trouble with rock falls."

"That's the place," Cooper said.

I climbed on, smelling the sea again. I'd been here once before. With a girl. The spot for which I was headed was a rock ridge in the coastal range slightly higher than its fellows. It was a half mile in through the brush from a small road winding north by northeast from a point halfway through Topanga Canyon. The sheer cliff that

Cooper had mentioned rose from the west shoulder of U.S. 101 on the right-hand side of the road as you headed north toward Frisco. By car U.S. 101 was a good seven miles away. Straight down the cliff it was only a little better than two thousand feet.

From the top of the cliff you could see for miles in all directions. While we had eaten our lunch, the girl and I had discussed the possibility of an agile man descending the cliff. She'd said it couldn't be done. I'd thought that I could do it. I'd know in a few minutes.

We'd been on level ground for some time now. Flagle quickened his steps in suspicion. His fingers bit into my shoulder. "Just a minute, Nelson. There are no caves up here. What are you trying to pull?"

I turned and faced him. The next nearest man, a San Mateo County trooper, was fifteen feet back of Flagle. The other men were strung out behind the trooper, their flashlights and lanterns giant fireflies hobbling up the rock.

I drove my fist into Flagle's stomach.

He staggered back into the trooper. I raced for the lip of the cliff. On the edge of it, I looked back. In the light of Flagle's electric lantern I could see that the trooper had drawn his gun. Flagle was standing with both hands pressed to his stomach. As I watched him, he gasped:

"Don't just stand there. Shoot him."

A bullet smacked into the trunk of the gnarled live-oak tree beside which I was standing. I went on over the cliff, too fast, my legs churning, trying to dig in with my heels, starting a series of miniature rock slides as I skidded into space.

I caught at an outcropping of sage. It pulled out by the roots. I caught at some greasewood. It held, twisting me in air, slamming me down on my belly at the edge of a twenty-foot drop.

A dozen flashlights stabbed down the cliff. Sheriff Cooper swore.

"The fool can't possibly make it. He'll break his neck. But just in case—you, Harris. Johnson. Highball it back to the cars and get down below there as fast as you can."

A bullet ricocheted off the rock, too close. I eased my body over the drop, hung on with my fingers, and let go. I landed in a crouch and rolled to break my fall, but I rolled too far, the momentum of my body propelling me down another steep series of slopes to wind up wedged between the cliff and the trunk of a live oak growing out into space.

I lay for a long time, breathless, trying to force myself to move, afraid. Then I realized that while the men on top of the cliff could hear me, they couldn't see me because of the outcropping. They were shouting at sounds. I could afford to be cautious now.

I lay a moment longer looking down at the speeding cars on U.S. 101. They looked like toys, with Christmas-tree bulbs for headlights. Beyond them was a necklace of lights formed by the beach houses of Malibu.

I unwedged myself and felt for toe- and handholds. Occasionally I found a chimney or a split where I could use my back. The last three hundred feet were the hardest. I inched down them, clinging to the rock like a fly. I thought twice the wind was going to blow me off. My fingers grew numb with strain. The muscles in my legs began to jerk. Then I was at the foot of the cliff, leaning against the rock, not knowing how much time had passed, not caring much, sick with simultaneous fear and relief.

When I could, I staggered across the highway in a lull between cars to the dubious shelter of a narrow beach. I found a shallow pool in the sand left by the outgoing tide and washed the sweat and blood from my hands and face and hair. The clean uniform I'd put on was powdered with rock dust. Both knees of my pants were torn.

I made myself as decent as I could. Then I limped south down the beach toward the neon sign of a bar. When I reached the bar I cut back to the highway, standing in just enough light to be seen, giving every car headed south the thumb.

The seventh car stopped. An omen? "Where to, mate?" the driver asked.

I said, "How far you going?"

"Dago," he said.

I said, "Swell," and got in, keeping my manacled hand in my right coat pocket.

The lad who'd picked me up eased his car into gear. "Passenger or freighter, mate?"

I said, "Freighter." I was still breathing hard. "How come you stopped for me? You do a hitch in the merchant marine?"

He laughed self-consciously. "You guessed it. In the port captain's office in Pedro. I had a very dangerous job. I ran an L. C. Smith."

I wished he would drive faster. I wanted to get back to the Purple Parrot before the law did. I wanted to push him out of the car and take over the wheel. I laughed, politely. "The paper work has to be done." He said, "Yeah. I guess so."

He drove a little faster. The tires made a nice sound on the pavement. I let him do the talking.

He said, "Fifty times I bet you I hoofed one-o-one to L.A. I mean during the war. Some folks would pick up sailors or marines. Some would pick up soldiers. But to hell with the merchant marine. Only once I got picked up. Then the guy was a fairy. So the day it all wound up, I said to myself any time I pass a real sailor I hope I should have a flat tire."

I settled back on the seat. "This is a break, fellow. Thanks. You live in Dago?"

He said, "That's right. I'm working out at the base. In a civilian capacity." He grinned sideways at me. "Get in a little rhubarb back there in that joint where I picked you up, mate?"

I grunted, "Yeah," and let it go at that. To prove what a tough sailor he'd been, he began a long story, with details, about a go-round he'd got into with a grease monkey from Lockheed.

I rode only half listening to him, just enough to grunt in the proper places, thinking about Corliss.

"Please. Don't make me hate you, Swede," she'd said. "Don't spoil something that may be very beautiful for both of us. I have a distinct aversion to being forced. When I go to bed with you, if I do, this time it's for keeps."

That was for sure. Then there was the business about the iron. Corliss *said* she'd washed and ironed my clothes, but it had been Mamie who had the burn. I might have known. I should have known. There'd been warning buoys and shoal markers all over the place. But I hadn't been able to see them for all that golden hair.

I knew now why Wally and Meek had laughed at me. They had reason to laugh. I might, or I might not, get away with killing Lippy Saltz, alias Jerry Wolkowysk. But body or no body, Corliss was my baby. Corliss was pinned on me.

I tried to remember the technical term. I couldn't. But I remembered reading of a similar case where a husband had been convicted of and executed for the murder of his wife without a corpus delicti. The court had accepted what it had called reasonable proof of death.

I drew up the indictment against me.

Corliss and I had quarreled. She'd told me to get out. She'd told me she was through, in front of witnesses. I was known to have a temper. I was out on bail for hitting one man too hard. I had been drunk for four days. We'd left the Purple Parrot together. I'd been arrested five hours later, ninety miles away. With a discharged gun, Corliss' car, and her bloodstained clothes in my possession. The blood on the clothes and in the back of the car checked with her known blood classification. Corliss had disappeared. If that didn't add up to reasonable proof of death, there weren't thirty-two points of the compass.

The lad driving finished his story. "So I hit him. With all I had, see? And brother, I mean I knocked him for a loop."

He realized he'd done all the talking and coughed, suddenly self-conscious.

"How did you make out in *your* fight, mate?"

"I lost my cap," I told him.

Chapter Nineteen

We passed through Balboa, then Corona Del Mar. The lad driving asked if I wanted to stop for a beer. I could have used one. I said, "No."

He shrugged and crawled into a shell of silence. As we rounded the bend near Laguna Beach, the headlights of his car picked up the barn of the roadhouse where Lippy Saltz had laid low. He wasn't being missed. There was a new night man back of the bar. The Beachcomber was still doing business. Men were bellied to the wood, wanting whisky, wanting women. Couples were dancing to the music of the juke box. But Lippy Saltz, alias Jerry Wolkowysk, was fish food. Battered chum. Possibly somewhere out in the Pacific in the belly of a shark, or wedged in the kelp with the crabs working on him, the quarter of a million dollars he'd got in the Palmer affair not doing him a bit of good.

It was suddenly hot in the car. I asked my host if I could roll down the window on my side.

He said, "Of course."

We were making good time now. Oceanside, Carlsbad, Encinitas grew out of the fog in a blur of haloed lights, then dropped behind us.

I sat straighter in the seat. I doubted if Sheriff Cooper or Captain Marks would reason I'd double back. They'd be more apt to figure that I'd either gone on up the coast or holed up in L.A. But the chances were they'd set up a roadblock in Palm Grove just in case I should head for Mexico.

"Cigarette?" my host asked.

I took one, careful to use my left hand, having a little trouble getting the cigarette out of the pack.

He was sympathetic. "What's the matter, mate? You bust your other hand in that fight back there?"

"It bothers me," I admitted. I used the lighter on the dash. "Let me out just this side of those spotlighted palm trees, please."

He stopped the car a hundred yards above the Purple Parrot. "What's the idea? I thought you were going to Dago."

"Did I say so?"

He thought back. "No."

I opened the door of the car. "I merely asked how far *you* were going. Anyway, thanks. Thanks a lot for the ride."

He sat looking at the hand he couldn't see. "You're welcome, I'm certain," he said. Then he fed gas to the car too fast, forgetting to shift into low, bucking it down 101, probably thanking his lucky stars, thinking, That guy has a gun in his pocket.

I watched the taillights of his car climb the hill beyond the Purple Parrot. Then I limped down the shoulder of the road.

Cooper hadn't bothered to leave a stake-out. There were no cars in front of the bar. Even Wally's beaten-up Ford was gone. The ceiling and the side lights in the bar were out but the night light was on.

I looked in through one of the front windows. Meek was alone in the bar. He was sitting on a stool looking into the bottom of an empty glass as if he wished he could fill it again but didn't dare.

As I watched him, the phone on the end of the bar rang. Meek climbed down off the stool and answered it. He listened intently a moment. Then, after speaking a few monosyllabic sentences into the mouthpiece, he cradled the phone and stood patting his face and neck with a soiled handkerchief. I was glad to know he had one. It would be something to stuff down his throat after he and I had finished our talk.

I didn't have much time. If there was a roadblock in Palm Grove, the lad who had picked me up would tell the officers about his seaman hitchhiker who had kept his hand in his coat pocket. The officers at the block would radio Cooper on their two-way. After that it would be a matter of minutes until the highway was filled with sirens.

I gripped the sill with my fingers, debating talking to Mamie first. She should be sober by now. What Mamie knew, she would tell me. I'd have to beat whatever I got out of Meek.

Meek took the decision out of my hands by scuttling out the side door of the bar and crunching across the gravel to the office cottage.

I walked around the back of the bar to come at the cottage from its blind side. The grass on both sides of the path was wet with fog and dew. Here in the pocket at the foot of the hill the night air was hot and humid. The smell of the flowers was almost overpowering. The crickets and the cicadas were a full-scale orchestra.

I cut through between Cottages 4 and 5. The couple in Number 4 was still awake, still arguing in the dark. Her voice was shrilly insistent. His was heavy with fatigue.

As I passed their open window she said, "I still think we ought to have told the officers what we saw when we drove in last night."

He said something about being on a vacation.

She wanted to know what difference that made.

"All right. All right," he conceded. "We'll tell them in the morning. Now for God's sake shut up and let me get some sleep."

I started on, then turned back on impulse and tried the screen door of their porch. The screen was unhooked. I opened it and crossed the porch and rapped softly on the closed door of the cottage proper.

"Who's there?" the man demanded.

I lied, "An officer. Please don't be alarmed and please don't light your light. But this is the second time you folks have been overheard discussing something you're con-cealing from the law. What is it?"

I hoped I sounded like an officer.

The woman said, "See? I told you."

He padded across the asphalt tile and opened the door. "O.K. Maybe we should have told you."

"Told us what?"

He padded back to the bed for his cigarettes.

She said, "What we saw when we drove in last night."

He came back to the door lighting a cigarette.

I said curtly, "Your names, please?"

She joined him in the doorway, struggling into a dres-sing gown. "Mr. and Mrs. Joseph Lewis of Carbondale,

Illinois. We're on our vacation. And we came all the way from Salt Lake City yesterday."

He blew smoke past my face. "Seven hundred and thirty-eight miles. That's the most we ever made in one day."

I couldn't see either of their faces. She sounded as if her lips were pursed. "And when Joe and I drove in last night, a little after midnight, we saw something I think you officers ought to know. You *are* investigating a murder?"

I said, "We are. What did you see?"

Mrs. Lewis said, "A naked woman."

"Where? In what cottage?"

"In Cottage Number One."

"What was she doing?"

"She was lying on the bed."

"This naked woman was alive?"

Lewis laughed. "Very much so. It was rare, believe me, Officer. We wondered what kind of joint we'd stumbled into."

I swallowed my heart. "Suppose you start at the beginning and tell me everything you saw."

Mrs. Lewis unpursed her lips. "Well, it was midnight. Perhaps a few minutes after midnight when we saw the vacancy sign. Like Joe told you, we'd driven seven hundred and thirty-eight miles and we were beat. So we parked in front of the office unit next door and rang the bell. We rang it several times. Then, when no one came to the door, we walked across the court toward the only other light we could see, hoping to find the manager, too tired to push on. It was then we saw the girl."

She pursed her lips again. "The blinds were closed but up an inch from the sill, enough so we could see the girl distinctly. We could also see the man."

"Describe him."

She said, "I'm afraid I can't. His back was to us."

"Was he a big man or a little man?"

"A big man. Rather fat."

"How was he dressed?"

"He wasn't. He was as naked as the girl."

Lewis laughed again. "I tell you, it was rich, Officer. The girl don't want to, see. She's lying on the bed crying like her heart is broken. But he keeps pestering her, feeling this and that. And, well, finally she just lets him have it. Like it don't mean a damn to her one way or another. And all the time he's doing it, she goes right on crying."

Mrs. Lewis said primly, "There's no need for you to be so graphic, Joe."

"What happened then?" I asked. "I mean, what did you folks do?"

Lewis said, "Well, by that time Eve was tugging at my shirttail. She said, "This is no place for us. So we walked back to the car and I was about to drive on when a little guy in blue dungarees came out of the bar and said he was the manager and did we want a cottage. And so help me, by then I was so beat I didn't care what kind of a joint it was."

"You told him what you'd seen?"

Mrs. Lewis said, "Certainly not. I don't know about California, but back in Carbondale we don't discuss such things. We merely told him we wanted to rent a unit. And we did. Although if Joe hadn't been so tired, I certainly would have insisted on driving on until we found another court with a vacancy."

Lewis added, "Shortly after that, maybe ten or fifteen minutes later, the cottage in which we'd seen the girl went dark and someone came out and drove away. We couldn't tell if it was the girl or the man. Then today we heard that the girl who owns these cottages was killed last night and that she lived in Cottage Number One. So Eve thought we ought to tell you fellows what we'd seen."

I said, "I'm glad you did."

He asked, "Who killed her? Her husband?"

I said, "That's the supposition. Was the girl a blonde or a brunette?"

"She was a blonde."

"Natural?"

"Decidedly."

"Pretty?"

"Very."

"And it was what time when you saw her?"

"After midnight. Say between fifteen after and half past." Lewis shifted his cigarette to his other band. "Does the information help you any?"

"Yes," I said. "It helps a lot. Thanks for telling me."

Mrs. Lewis was tardily suspicious. "What's your name, Officer?"

I walked off the porch without answering her and waded the wet grass to the office cottage. The door was shut. The Venetian blinds were closed. Mamie was crying. I stood straddling a wedge of light leaking out from under a blind, listening to Meek lay down the law.

He said, "I haven't told you anything. I'm not going to. What you don't know you can't tell. If the deal levels off the way I hope it will, it means a nice piece of change for me. And God knows I can use it. You think I *like* to mess around dirt?"

Mamie sobbed, "But if Swede—"

"Swede, Swede, Swede," Meek mimicked her. "That's all you've been able to think about since the big square-head first showed up." Liquid gurgled as someone drank from a bottle.

Mamie cried even harder.

Meek sounded as if he was pacing the floor. "You'd have wised off again this afternoon and maybe queered the whole thing if I hadn't passed you out. Next time I'll give you so many pills you won't come out of it."

"I don't care what you do," Mamie sobbed.

I walked around to the front of the cottage. The screen on the porch was unhooked. The inside door was locked. I turned the knob and put my shoulder to it. The door opened with a rasp of metal being torn out of wood.

Mamie was sitting on the rumpled bed. Her hair was disordered. Her make-up was streaked with tears. Her eyes were puffed with seconal. When she saw me she sat straight on the bed and her breasts thrust upward against the thin silk of her only garment. The back of one small white hand brushed hair and tears from her eyes. Her lips parted. She screamed:

"Swede!"

Meek dropped the pint of whisky he was holding and tried to climb the wall. His scrawny chest labored. His eyes darted from side to side like a trapped rat trying to find a taut hawser he could use to desert a sinking ship.

Mamie screamed again. "Swede!"

Between the noise I'd made breaking down the door and Mamie's screams, lights were springing on in the dark units around the court. Lewis and his wife walked out on their porch. I heard him say, "What the hell?"

Meek was still trying to climb the wall. "Get out of here," he squealed. "Get out of here, you dirty killer."

I took another step toward him. He stopped trying to climb the wall and flicked open a four-inch switch blade, holding it with his knuckles up and the handle pressed against his belly.

I could hear voices on the drive now. In the distance a siren began to undulate. There'd been a roadblock in Palm Grove. The former merchant marine who had picked me up had talked.

Meek's lips were flecked with fear froth. "Don't you dare touch me. If you do I'll tell Sheriff Cooper you killed Jerry Wolkowysk and drove his car over that cliff."

He jabbed at me with the knife. I slapped him away from the wall and up against the dresser. "I'm not interested in Wolkowysk. I know where he is. Where's Sophia?"

Mamie got to her feet.

"What did you say?" Meek gasped.

I repeated. "I asked you where Sophia was. You know. Sophia Palanka. My wife."

Chapter Twenty

The Mission Hotel was well named. Most of the couples who checked in were looking for something. It was on the fringe of the Mexican district, not far from San Diego's version of Skid Row.

I parked the Chrysler with Illinois plates in front of a bar across the street and looked at the hotel for a moment. The sidewalk in front of it was crowded with sailors and their girls and sailors who wished they had girls. As I watched, an alert shore patrol walked by.

I glanced in the rear-vision mirror of my borrowed car. Outside of the blood on my right coat sleeve and the general pummeling I'd taken, I didn't look too bad. I looked like the first mate of a freighter who had been on a hell of a binge.

The bar in front of which I was parked was crowded with sailors. I walked in and bought a drink and a package of cigarettes with the tuck-away twenty I always keep folded in my watch pocket.

The barman was used to sailors. "Been in a fight, mate?" he asked.

I nodded over the rum.

The barman looked at my sleeve. "Her husband came home too soon, huh? Looks like he used a knife on you."

I finished the drink and set the glass back on the wood. "Yeah. But you ought to see him."

He laughed as he mopped at a puddle of spilled beer. I tore the package of cigarettes open with my teeth and lighted one.

The San Diego police were on the job. As I walked from the bar a radio prowl car parked in front of the green Chrysler, at an angle, effectively blocking it. A young officer got out of the police car with a clip board in one hand.

He looked at the plates on the Chrysler, then grinned at his partner. "Talk about service. This is the one that just came on the air. The green Chrysler with Illinois plates that guy Nelson borrowed at the Purple Parrot. Call in and tell Paddy we've found it."

The usual curious crowd began to form. I walked across the street and into the lobby of the Mission Hotel.

A young desk clerk was checking the entries at Santa Anita. He put his Racing Form aside. "Yes, sir?"

I laid down one of the fives the barman had given me in change. "I'd like a room. With or without bath. It doesn't matter. But preferably on the fifth floor."

The clerk pushed a registration card at me. "Yes, sir." He laid a key on the counter. "That will be three-fifty." He gave me my change. "Had a little trouble, eh, mate?"

"Yeah. A little," I admitted. I kept my right hand in my pocket. "Sign the card for me, will you, fellow? Swen Nelson. Simmons Line. San Pedro."

"Sure thing, mate." He wrote the information on the card. "But that arm looks bad to me. Maybe you ought to see a doctor about it."

I said, "I intend to. Later."

I picked up my change and the key. In the elevator I

looked at the key for the first time. The tag on it read 519. I asked the pretty Mexican girl running the cage if Room 519 was in the front or the back of the hotel.

She stopped the cage on the fifth floor and graciously pointed down the hall. "Five-nineteen is at the end of the hall, *señor*. In the back. You cannot possibly miss it."

I thanked her and walked down the hall in the direction she'd pointed until she'd closed the cage door. Then I stopped and looked at the numbers. The room I wanted was in the front of the hotel.

I leaned against the wall and lighted a fresh cigarette from the butt of the one that was burning my fingers. Most of the transoms along the hall were lighted and open. The voices I could hear were young. Listening to them gave me a funny feeling. Behind the closed doors couples were loving, quarreling, making up, worrying about money, his job, her health, happy to be together. Living.

The hall smelled like all cheap hotel hallways. I tried to take my right hand out of my pocket. I couldn't. Meek had done a good job with his knife.

I pushed my back away from the wall and walked down the faded runner toward the window I could see in the front of the hotel. The window was open. There was a red light over it. I looked out and down. The fire-escape platform was square with a hole in it next to the wall and a rusted iron ladder running down through the hole to the next square landing.

For a man with two hands it was an easy swing from the fire-escape platform to the sill of the front window with the drawn shade. With one hand I didn't dare chance it. It was five floors down to the sidewalk.

There was a light in 501, but the shade was drawn and the transom was closed. I could hear a splashing of water back of the shade.

I looked across the street at the green Chrysler I'd borrowed. Without the owner's permission. From Mr. and Mrs. Joseph Lewis of Carbondale, Illinois. There was an even bigger crowd around it now. The two prowl-car cops, augmented by two plain-clothes men, were fanning through the crowd asking questions. When he next put his feet under the poker table in the back room of the Elks Club in Carbondale, Lewis would have quite a story to toss in the pot with his ante.

I heard a faint *snick* behind me. As if someone had closed a door, trying to be quiet about it. I swung around and sat on the sill, breathing hard. All the closed doors in the hall looked the same.

I stood up and rapped on the door of Room 501.

The faint sound of running water stopped. There was a moment of silence. Then Wally asked, "Who is it?"

I tossed my cigarette out the open window. "It isn't Western Union."

A key turned in the lock. The door opened. Wally thrust a gun into my stomach. "Come in."

I walked into the room and closed the door.

Wally leaned even harder on the gun. "How did you get away from the cops? How did you know we were here?"

I said, "Meek told me. Under protest. In fact, we had quite a go-around about it, during which Mamie took a knife thrust that was intended for me. I just left her in the emergency room at the hospital with two nurses and an intern. She may live. She may not."

I looked past Wally at Corliss. She was standing in front of the washbasin in the bathroom holding a glass of brown dye over a mop of wet brown hair. Her mouth was open but no sound was coming out. All she had on was a sheer slip liberally splattered with dye. She was even prettier as a brunette than she had been blonde.

"You can't dye it all, honey," I told her. "In your line of business the dye will wear off where it matters. But I'll bet you looked cute as hell with red hair."

She dropped the glass. "You know."

I leaned against the door. "That you're Sophia Palanka?" I nodded. "Yes. That probably was Yugoslav the lad in the bar in Tijuana was spitting at you. Who was he? An old admirer?"

Corliss came to the door of the bathroom. "He'd seen me dance."

"That's a new name for it," Wally said.

Corliss looked at him, then back at me. "Who knows you're here, Swede?"

"You and me, baby," I told her. "What's the matter? You don't seem very glad to see me."

She chewed at her underlip. "I'm not."

"What you keeping your hand in your pocket for?" Wally asked. "You got a gun in there?"

I pointed the handcuff at him. "What do you think?"

The big barman began to sweat. As I'd sweated for four days. "I knew you were up to something when you confessed to the cops and offered to lead them to Corliss' body. I figured you were going to try a break.

But I didn't think you'd be dumb enough to double back."

I shifted my weight from one foot to the other. "What did you expect me to do? Go up to San Quentin, take three deep breaths, and say, 'Good morning, Warden. My name is Swen Nelson. I'm a seaman. That is, I used to be a seaman. I'd been at sea, off and on, for eighteen years when I decided I'd wasted enough of my life. So I started for Hibbing, Minnesota, to buy a farm and get married and settle down. Maybe even have a half-dozen kids. But I went on a binge instead. During it I met a girl. The girl I'd been looking for all my life.' " I looked at Corliss. " 'I loved her on sight. I—still love her. I'll always love her. Even if she didn't turn out to be all I thought she was.' "

Corliss began to cry.

"Don't listen to him," Wally said. "He's just trying to make trouble between us."

Still looking at Corliss, I asked, "Has Connors been in on this from the start?"

Corliss stopped crying. Her lower lip thrust out in its familiar pout. "No," she said coldly. "Oh, he and Meek have known for some time I wasn't all I pretended to be. They've been chiseling pennies from me for a year. But all they were doing was guessing until Palmer's body was found and Mr. Green came to the court with the information that Jerry Wolkowysk was really Lippy Saltz. Then they both cut themselves in." Corliss made a gesture of distaste. "Wally all the way last night." Her voice was small. She refused to meet my eyes. "Because he knew no matter how badly I felt about you, I didn't dare refuse him." She squeezed her wet hair to the back of her head and held it there. Her voice was barely audible. "Because I'd been living a lie. Because I wasn't Corliss Mason. Because I was Sophia Palanka and the F.B.I. wants me— for murder."

Connors was smug. "That's right. If you'll pardon the expression, Nelson, I cut myself a piece of cake. I liked it. And I'm going to keep right on cutting. Corliss and I are taking the midnight plane to Frisco. From there we're flying to Bogotá. To hell with the Purple Parrot. Let Meek have it."

"The hell you say," I said.

I hit him with my left hand. So hard his pig eyes filled with desperation. He sucked in his fat guts against the shot he expected. From the gun I didn't have. Then, almost slyly, he raised the gun in his hand. I knocked it across the room and under the bed. Then I got my right hand out of my pocket and swung it. My numbed fist missed his face. The handcuff didn't. His broken jaw gaped. He started to scream in agony. Before he could make much noise I swung my fist again, this time to his head. He went down like a poled steer.

Corliss hadn't moved. She was still clutching her wet hair to her neck. It gave her an oddly foreign look.

I yelled at her. "Don't just stand there. Get dressed. The police were on their way to the Purple Parrot when I beat this address out of Meek. I stole a car to get here. The car is parked across the street with four smart San Diego cops asking questions about it right now. 'Did you see the sailor who parked it? Where did he go?' And I'm wanted for murder, remember? For killing you. Don't stand there looking at me. Get dressed. In just about four minutes every cop in Southern California is going to bust in here."

Her white breasts strained against the sheer silk of her dye-spotted slip. "Why should I get dressed?"

I told her. "I'm taking you out of here."

"Where?"

"I don't know. We'll have to figure that out. Anywhere you'll be safe."

"You mean you want me to escape?"

"I do."

"Even if I am—bad?"

"Even so."

Corliss laid a small hand on my chest. Her eyes searched mine. "After what I did and tried to do to you?"

"After what you did and tried to do to me."

"Why?"

"Maybe because I love you." I tilted her chin. "Why did you cry last night?" I quoted Mr. Lewis. "As if your heart was broken."

Her wet eyes continued to search mine. "Maybe because I love you. Maybe because I was ashamed. Maybe because I wanted to be what I'd pretended to be. Instead of what I am." She cried quietly. "Maybe because I wished I had been born in a small town and had married a rich man's son. So he could die like the one I made up did and leave me free to marry you." Corliss buried her cheek against my chest and sobbed. "Instead of being a cheap little South Chicago strip-teaser who listened to Lippy Saltz."

Her hand was still on my chest. I kissed the tips of her fingers, then her wet hair. "Get dressed, little sweetheart," I whispered. "We'll thrash this all out later. *If* we make it."

Corliss looked into my eyes again. "You really want me to, Swede? You care that much?"

"I do."

She took a deep breath. Her lower lip quivered. "Then, whatever you say, Swede."

She rinsed her hair in the basin, then toweled it with her eyes closed, her lips moving as if she was praying. Then she peeled off her sodden slip and stood nude and lovely a moment while she wrapped her dyed hair in a long white scarf, forming a smart white turban.

As she put on her silver sandals she asked, "How much time have we?"

I cracked the drawn shade and looked across the street. The four San Diego policemen were standing beside the police car comparing notes. As I watched, one of the plainclothes men looked across the street into the lobby of the hotel.

I said tersely, "Minutes. But I think we still can make it if we can slip out the back way."

I turned from the window. Corliss had pulled a simple white dress over the turban and was reaching her camel's hair coat from the closet. With a fringe of brown hair showing under the turban, she didn't even resemble Corliss Mason. She looked smart and expensive and foreign.

As I started for the door she picked an equally smart overnight case from the floor of the clothes closet and caught at my arm as I passed her.

"Please," she said simply. "Kiss me for luck, Swede. So I'll know."

I kissed her. For a long time. Then I released her. "Now do you know?"

Her eyes shining, she nodded. "Yes."

She was nearest the door. She opened it and started out, and stopped as Green blocked the doorway.

"Hello, Sophia," he said quietly. "Going somewhere?"

Corliss whimpered like a kicked puppy. Her nostrils distended. She slammed the door in Green's face and raced for the open window, screaming at me.

"Goddamn you, Swede. You tricked me. You meant to turn me in to the law all the time." She ripped the drawn shade from the window. "That's why you wanted to get me out of the room. You meant to have me arrested."

She straddled the sill, her skirt sliding high on her thigh as Green pushed the slammed door open. Corliss continued to curse me.

"You big lousy Swede. From Hibbing, Minnesota. You goddamn no-good bastard." But her eyes didn't match her words. Corliss' eyes were shining as brightly as they had when I'd kissed her, when she'd said now she knew.

"No! Don't try it," Green warned her from the doorway.

Her eyes still caressing me, Corliss reached for the fire-escape ladder with one hand and swung her slim body into space.

She screamed as her coat caught on a projecting nail. She tried to free it with the hand still clutching the overnight bag. As she did, her left hand let go of the rusted iron ladder, and before either Green or I could reach her she fell backward into space, her terror filling the night with screams.

I watched from the window, sick. Her body turned over and over. Her outflung arm struck the railing of the landing on the third floor. The overnight case sprang open. And all the money in the world spilled out and formed a fluttering green umbrella over her falling body.

Green leaned against the windowsill. "The crazy little fool," he breathed. "She might have known."

Chapter Twenty-One

The office of the Federal Bureau in San Diego was small but comfortable. Softly spoken, well-dressed, efficient counterparts of Green spoke into phones, made notes, or just sat looking pleased.

Captain Marks and Flagle and Sheriff Cooper and Harris were there. So were Mr. and Mrs. Lewis. So was Wally. So was Meek. Wally had a towel tied around his jaw. Meek's head was bandaged.

A doctor worked on my arm as Green talked.

"You get the setup now, Nelson?" he asked.

I said, "Most of it, I think. Corliss was acting a part. She played me for a sucker."

Green nodded, well pleased with Green. "That's right. The girl you knew and married as Corliss Mason was in reality Sophia Palanka, a former entertainer and strip-teaser in a South Chicago night club." Green lighted a cigarette. "The club was patronized mainly by Yugoslavs and Poles and Bohemians, men from the neighboring steel mills. But now and then a party of 'slummers' dropped in. That's probably how she met Phillip E. Palmer the Third."

I fought a desire to be sick.

"Am I hurting you?" the doctor asked.

"Not too bad," I told him.

Green continued. "As yet we haven't been able to

locate her family. It's really immaterial now. Probably the usual background. A broken home or a drunken stepfather. The kid wanted some of the pretties of life and set out to get them, by any means she could. With her looks and body, that was easy. Up to a point."

The doctor finished with my arm. "Let it rest for a few days, mate. The knife went right through the muscle so it will probably be stiff for a while. But no permanent damage has been done."

I lowered my hand to my lap and let the handcuff dangle between my legs. "Thanks. Thanks a lot."

Green snuffed the cigarette he was smoking. "There is a lot of the background we still don't know and probably never will. We do know the Palmer affair was carefully planned. During the entire time she worked at the club, Sophia was a redhead. More, unlike most girls in her profession, she never, to our knowledge, had any pictures taken of herself. All we had to go on was a blurred glossy print of Sophia and Phillip E. Palmer the Third taken on their wedding night, by a night-club photographer, both of them stewed to the gills and Sophia looking away from the camera. In fact, it wasn't until we located one of her more intimate customers that we realized her red hair might not be natural."

One of Green's fellow agents who had been talking to Washington on the phone hung up, clasped his hands, and shook them at Green. Because a girl named Sophia Palanka was dead.

Green continued. "We don't even know the exact date that she tied in with Lippy. But we know that she did, and we have reason to believe that for some months before the Palmer affair they lived together under a mutual-agreement relationship. Of course, what made it so difficult for us was that the case was three years old before we were called in. As murders go, it was clever. If Palmer's body hadn't been found by a party of city slickers hunting ducks in a slough where there haven't been any ducks for fifty years, the State Department would still be demanding that Phillip E. Palmer the Third be returned from behind the Iron Curtain. Because to all intents and purposes Phillip E. Palmer the Third and his blushing bride dropped out of sight in Bucharest. And neither of them was ever seen again."

"Are you positive," Flagle asked, "that Corliss Mason and this Sophia Palanka were the same girl?"

Green nodded. "Positive. We have been for some hours. Ever since Washington reported that some of the fingerprints the San Mateo technicians took off the car Nelson was driving when he was arrested matched the prints of a thumb and second finger, both of them apparently feminine, that we took off the night-club picture of Palmer and his bride." Green grinned at Captain Marks. "That's why I wasn't too much interested in your case against Nelson or his confession that he had killed his wife. It was too pat a solution. Besides, by then I had my eye on Connors. For a barman in a roadside bar, he was just too good to be true."

Wally glowered at him over the towel holding his broken jaw together.

"As you gentlemen know," Green said, "in most of these cases it's the little things that lead to their solution."

I sat looking at the dangling handcuff. The little

things. Fingerprints on a forgotten night-club picture. A former carnival barker snitching a quick drink instead of being on deck to rent a cottage to Mr. and Mrs. Joseph Lewis of Carbondale, Illinois.

Green continued. "When we were called in on the case we were in error in not realizing Sophia and Lippy were as smart as they were. And they were smart. For one thing, they must have dickered to buy the Purple Parrot months before they murdered Palmer, thus confusing the time element completely. Then they only paid twenty-five thousand down, meeting the monthly payments out of income, leaving them"—Green corrected himself—"leaving her almost the entire sum they got from Palmer intact, for getaway money, in case something like this happened."

Sheriff Cooper said, "Leaving *her?* You boys are certain, then, that Saltz, alias Jerry Wolkowysk, is dead?"

Green looked at me. With thoughtful speculation in his eyes. "Y-yes. Fairly so, Sheriff. As I see it, Lippy had served his purpose, and I imagine the little blonde saw to it that Lippy was in his car when it went over the cliff. He was a loose end that needed tying. He could identify her as his partner in the killing. He also undoubtedly claimed the greatest share of the money, not realizing he had been used, as Sophia used every man with whom she came in contact. Yes. I think we're safe in assuming Saltz is dead. How about it, Nelson? Can you tell us anything about Wolkowysk?"

I looked him in the eye. "No, sir."

"You're positive?"

I looked at Wally and Meek. Neither of them dared to

talk. This way they were merely hangers-on. If they talked, if they admitted they had been bleeding Corliss, they automatically tagged themselves with an accessory-after-the-fact charge. No. I was safe enough as far as either of them was concerned. All they wanted now was to get out with as much skin as they could.

"Yeah. I'm positive," I said.

So what could Green prove without a body? I pushed my luck by tapping the handcuff and looking at Captain Marks.

"Now, how about the jewelry? If you're convinced by now I didn't kill my wife, how's for taking this thing off?"

So what could he say? He was sorry?

Captain Marks unlocked the metal and put the handcuffs in his pocket. His face was red. He cleared his throat. I blocked his apology.

"Forget it."

Captain Marks nodded his thanks. Then he asked Green, "Just where did Nelson come in?"

Green said, "As a patsy, a fall guy. Sophia needed someone to kill her. As I see her, she must have been a bit of a sadist."

A bee buzzing on a windshield. *Plop*.

"She knew we'd catch up with her, eventually. So when they read in the papers that Palmer's body had been found and their perfect murder had a big flaw in it, she sold Lippy a bill of goods. She persuaded him to find a man to 'kill' her." Green got even with me for refusing to tell the truth about Wolkowysk. "Someone not too smart. Someone without any family ties. Someone with his heart below his waist. Someone like Nelson. A sailor with a tart in every port from here to Mozambique. A man who'd fall hard for the sweet young thing she was pretending to be, a chaste yet passionate young widow. That about right, Nelson?"

I nodded at him. "Right."

Flagle said, "I get it. With Saltz in the ocean, Mrs. Nelson presumed to be dead, and Nelson gone to the gas chamber for her murder, she would have disappeared as completely as Phillip E. Palmer the Third."

Green nodded, still looking at me. "It may interest you to know that we've done considerable checking on you, Nelson. And James Ginty, the San Pedro agent of the line you've sailed with for years, gives you a very clean ticket, mister."

I said, "Thanks," tight-lipped.

"He says you're a hell-raising squarehead on shore. An overaged juvenile delinquent with a lot of screwball ideas, the last of which was quitting the sea and buying a farm somewhere in Minnesota. But he also says that afloat you're one of the best officers the line ever had, levelheaded, dependable, sober. And Ginty asked me to tell you, if you were off your binge, that the Sally B. was delayed in port, and you can take her out if you're willing to sail as skipper."

I got to my feet. "Thanks a lot for telling me. Now would you tell me one last thing?"

"Possibly."

"How did you know Corliss was in Room Five-o-one of the Mission Hotel?"

Green smiled. "That was an exceedingly difficult deduction on my part. I followed Connors when he left the Purple Parrot. I was ready to make the pinch, merely waiting to see if more of the crowd would show up, when you blundered in." Green transferred his attention to Meek. "What do you know about this, fellow?"

"Nothing," Meek said flatly. "I don't know a thing. I was just the gardener, see?"

Sheriff Cooper asked where Meek came in.

Green said, "Small fry. Possibly a Chicago acquaintance of Lippy's sponging up a few crumbs. But I seriously doubt if we can connect him. How's his wife making out?"

Cooper took off his hat. "Not too good the last time I heard. They think she's going to make the grade, but it will be a long pull. I guess he knifed her pretty bad, trying to get past her to Nelson."

Green lighted a cigarette. "Do the Bureau a favor, Sheriff. If Mrs. Meek shouldn't make it, the charge is obvious. But if she does pull through, book him for assault with a deadly weapon with intent to kill and see that he's tucked away for five or ten years. Will you do that, Sheriff?"

"I will," Cooper said.

"The same goes for Connors. But as he assaulted Nelson here in town, we'll let the San Diego police take care of him."

I asked, "How about me?"

Green blew smoke through his nose. "You're perfectly free to go, as far as we're concerned. But you can forget any interest you may think you have in the Purple Parrot because of your marriage to Sophia Palanka. That will go to the Palmer estate, as it was obviously bought with Palmer money."

I said, "That's fine with me. But how about the almost twelve grand I had on me when the San Mateo cops picked me up? That was my own money. And I can prove I had that much by Ginty."

"That's out of my hands," Green said.

Captain Marks cleared his throat. "If you'll drop into my office tomorrow morning, Nelson, I'll see that your personal property is returned." He took the engagement ring I'd given Corliss from an envelope. "All of it I have with me is the ring. And you can have that now."

I tried to put the ring on my finger. It wouldn't even start on. I dropped it in my pants pocket and looked at Sheriff Cooper. "How clean am I with you?"

He asked Mr. and Mrs. Lewis if they wanted to prefer charges against me for using their car.

Lewis was a good guy. He shook his head. "Under the circumstances, no."

"That's it, then," Cooper said. "You intend to ship out?"

I said I hadn't made up my mind.

He said, "Well, anyway, drop around to Palm Grove in the morning. I think I can persuade Farrell to give you a quick trial. That way we can fine you twenty-five dollars or so for popping Corado and return the five hundred you posted for bail."

I tried to grin. It came out sort of wry. "I'll be lousy with dough." I walked to the door, then turned back and asked what was on my mind. "Just one more thing. What happens to Corliss now?"

"What do you mean what happens to her?" Green asked.

"What happens to her body?"

Green seemed to understand. He said quietly, "You can claim it if you care to, Nelson. Do you?"

I nodded. "Yeah." I took the engagement ring from my pocket and laid it on his blotter. "Have someone put that on her finger, will you? I lost the other one. With my cap. Somewhere up around Malibu."

Then I walked out of the office in the deep silence that followed.

Chapter Twenty-Two

The hospital corridor smelled like all hospital corridors at three o'clock in the morning. I tiptoed after the nurse into the dimly lighted ward. At the foot of the bed, she said, "Now, only for a moment, Mr. Nelson. Mrs. Meek is a very sick girl."

I tiptoed around the screen. Mamie was lying facing the window. With her hair in long twin braids and her face scrubbed clean of make-up she looked about fifteen.

One small white hand was lying palm up on the spread. I stooped and kissed it. "Hello, baby. How goes it with you?"

She looked at my eyes, then out the window at the night. "All right, I guess," she said.

I drew up a chair and sat where she had to look at me. "Thanks. Thanks a lot, Mamie."

"You're welcome, I'm sure," she said. Her breasts moved under the sheet. "I heard one of the nurses talking. She said that Corliss is dead."

I instinctively reached for the cap I didn't have. "Yeah."

"What are you going to do now, Swede?"

I moved the chair closer to the bed, talking in a whisper so I wouldn't disturb the other women in the ward. I knew what Mamie wanted me to say. I wished that I could say it. "I'm going back to sea," I told her. "I just called Ginty and I'm sailing for Sydney tomorrow night. As skipper of the Sally B."

"Oh," Mamie said, without expression.

"But before I left, I wanted to talk to you."

She said listlessly, "About what?"

I took the little white palm and held it to my cheek. "About the guy you used to think you'd meet someday. Remember?"

Her eyes got wet. "That was a long time ago."

I nodded. "That's right. Back in a little town in South Dakota. What's its name?"

Her voice still toneless, she said, "Murdock. Population, two thousand, four hundred and twenty-one."

I continued to fondle her hand. "How would you like to go back there, Mamie?"

She tried to shrug her bandaged shoulder and winced. "I suppose it's as good a place for me to be as any."

"Fine," I said. "Fine. I'll leave some money at the desk tomorrow afternoon. Quite a bit of money. Ten, eleven thousand dollars. Whatever I have left after doing what I can for Corliss. And when they let you out of here, you take the first train back to Murdock. Promise?"

The corners of her mouth turned down. "Why should you give me all that money?"

"Maybe I want to. Promise?"

Mamie's voice matched the dimly lighted corridor. "All right. What difference does it make?"

I kissed her fingertips, one by one. "A lot of difference. I had a dream, too, kid. Make it come true for me, will you? Get back in that old routine you told me about.

You know. A movie on Saturday night, church on Sundays and Wednesdays. And the first thing you know, the right guy's going to come along. And you're going to love him like you never loved anyone before in all your life. You can use the dough to buy a farm. And live happy. With this guy you're going to meet. Maybe have a half-dozen kids. Even name one of them Swen."

The hovering nurse said crisply, "You'll have to leave now, Mr. Nelson. The patient is very weak."

I kissed Mamie's lips. "Good-by, kid."

She closed her wet eyes as she kissed me back. Her voice was small. "Good-by, Swede."

Then I was out on the dark street again, walking along the waterfront, maybe saying a little prayer. For the woman I loved. Smelling familiar smells, hearing familiar sounds.

Smelling a new coiled hawser, tar, the sweet-sour smell of the flats, hearing a ship's bell strike the watch, hearing the suck of the tide around the pilings: the tide that waited for no man, knowing life would go on, as it has ever since the first amoeba was washed up out of the slime, a microscopic nucleated mass of protoplasm, and began to multiply.

The three words coming out of the dark made me turn my head to look at the girl standing under the street light.

"Hello, sailor. Lonely?"

Her lips were a smear of crimson. She was young. She was pretty. She was mine.

I tucked her hand under my arm. "Why, yes," I told her. "As it so happens, I am."

THE
END

Lawrence
BLOCK
Grifter's Game

Originally Published As 'MONA'

Con man Joe Marlin was used to scoring easy cash off gullible women. But that was before he met Mona Brassard — and found himself holding a stolen stash of raw heroin. Now Joe's got to pull off the most dangerous con of his career. One that will leave him either a killer — or a corpse. GRIFTER'S GAME was the first mystery novel multiple Edgar Award-winnner Lawrence Block published under his own name. It is now appearing for the first time under his original title.

"[The] one writer of mystery and detective fiction who comes close to replacing the irreplaceable John D. MacDonald."
— STEPHEN KING

Order at www.HardCaseCrime.com or call 1-800-481-9191 (10am to 9pm EST)
...Or Mail in This Handy Order Form:

Little Girl Lost

by **RICHARD ALEAS**

Miranda Sugarman was supposed to be in the Midwest, working as an eye doctor. *So how did she wind up dead on the roof of New York's seediest strip club?*

Ten years earlier, Miranda had been P.I. John Blake's girlfriend. Now he must uncover her secret life as a strip tease queen. But the deeper he digs, the deadlier the danger… until a shattering face-off in an East Village tenement changes his life forever.

LITTLE GIRL LOST is the stunning debut novel from Shamus Award-nominated RICHARD ALEAS, a writer whose stories have been selected for *Best Mystery Stories of the Year*. It features a brand new cover painting by legendary pulp artist Robert McGinnis, creator of the posters for *Breakfast at Tiffany's* and the original Sean Connery James Bond movies.

"[Aleas] gives Chandler a run for his money." — Paramour

The CONFESSION

By Two-Time Edgar Award Nominee

DOMENIC STANSBERRY

She was young, beautiful… and dead!

Jake Danser has it all: a beautiful wife, a house in the California hills, and a high-profile job as a forensic psychologist. But he's also got a mistress. And when she's found strangled to death with his necktie, the police show up at his door. Now it's up to Jake to prove he didn't do it. But how can he, when all the evidence says he did?

As Jake's life crumbles around him, he races to find proof of his innocence. And with every step, the noose is tightening…

PRAISE FOR THE BOOKS OF DOMENIC STANSBERRY:

"Stansberry does it with originality." — The New York Times
"A murky, moody slice of noir." — Kirkus Reviews
"Fascinating, beautifully written… an enviable achievement."
— San Francisco Chronicle